HATCHED
DRAGON FARMER

HATCHED
DRAGON FARMER

BOOK ONE

CAREN HAHN

Hatched: Dragon Farmer by Caren Hahn

Published by Seventy-Second Press

www.carenhahn.com

Copyright © 2022 Caren Hahn

Hardcover ISBN-13: 978-1-958609-04-0

Paperback ISBN-13: 978-1-7352272-9-0

Cover design by Andrew Hahn.

Edited by Rachel Pickett.

Printed in the USA

For Cathryn, without whom this story wouldn't exist.

BOOKS BY CAREN HAHN

ROMANTIC FANTASY:

*Find Caren's work
on Amazon.com*

THE WALLKEEPER TRILOGY

Burden of Power

Pain of Betrayal

Gleam of Crown

THE HATCHED TRILOGY

Hatched: Dragon Farmer

Hatched: Dragon Defender

Hatched: Dragon Speaker

CONTEMPORARY SUSPENSE:

This Side of Dark

What Comes After

THE OWL CREEK SERIES

Smoke over Owl Creek

Hunt at Owl Creek

Visit carenhahn.com to receive a free
copy of *Charmed: Tales from
Quarantine and Other Short Fiction.*

HATCHED
DRAGON FARMER

BOOK ONE

CAREN HAHN

SEVENTY-SECOND
PRESS

1

BROODY

Charl trotted down the lane as fast as she could in boots that were too big for her feet. They were Roland's old boots, but they kept out water better than her own, so she always wore them when doing chores. It wasn't as if her brother needed them anymore.

Her breath streamed out in a white mist as she hurried down the path, the chill air of an autumn morning making her nose run. But the sky was bright and clear, a glorious blue setting off the brilliant yellow leaves overhead, promising a warm afternoon.

As Praxton's farm came into view, Charl hoped he hadn't already left for the day. He'd been clearing timber on the mountain all week with his new team of mules, and if Charl was too late she'd have to wait another day to ask for his help.

To her relief, she spotted a figure in the tall grass down by the river as she emerged from the forest path. She veered off in that direction, slowing to a walk and wiping her nose on her sleeve.

Praxton was cutting the grass with a long scythe, making wide sweeping motions that looked effortless. Charl knew better. Whenever Charl cut the grass in the pasture—now that she no longer had any goats to keep it down—her shoulders ached for days.

Praxton's back was to her, so she gave him a wide berth as she approached. When she came round into his view, he stopped and looked up. Steam rose from his warm body in the early morning air, and Charl told herself she only casually noticed that although he wore no jacket against the chill, his shirt clung to his back with sweat. Surely the fluttering in her middle was from nothing more than her brisk walk.

"Morning, Charl. What brings you out here so early?" He leaned on the scythe and brushed his straw-colored hair off his forehead.

"Stella is broody."

"Again?"

Charl nodded.

Prax frowned. "I thought her breed wasn't supposed to—"

"I thought so too." Charl raised her hand to her eyes to shade them from the sun. It was just rising over the tops of the fir trees, blazing gold over the grass which lay long and dry from late summer heat. "Roland said she'd never been broody for him, but this is twice now this year."

Praxton looked over the unfinished field.

"It doesn't have to be today," Charl said apologetically. "Whenever you think you can spare the time. I wouldn't even ask if she didn't have such wicked talons."

Prax glanced at her forehead, looking at the pink scar that rested above her right eye. "How much longer are you going to try and run that place on your own, Charl? When do you decide it's too much?"

Charl pressed her lips together. "Roland practically took care of things by himself after our parents died, before I had learned enough to be of any use. If he can do it, so can I."

Prax raised an eyebrow. "Look, it's not my business. But if you ever have to put Stella or one of the others down, have you considered how hard that will be? It might be worth selling them now while they're still young and have lots of years of laying left."

Charl felt a flush of annoyance. "I'm not putting any of them down. Or selling them either. If you don't want to help, I'll take care of her myself. I've done it before." That was partly true. She'd succeeded in getting Stella off the nest and away from her eggs last time, but then Stella had attacked. Fortunately, it was just a warning. If she'd meant to do serious harm, Charl would have lost the eye.

"No need for that. I'll come. Should I bring the scythe?" Prax added with a wink.

Charl snorted. "Only if you want to lose an arm. Thanks, Prax. I owe you."

She waited while he hefted the scythe over his shoulder and walked back up to the barn to return it. Prax had made such improvements to this place since he'd moved here two years earlier. Charl's previous neighbors had been an old couple with no children and poor health. When Prax bought it, the thatch on the cottage was almost gone and raccoons were living in the chimney. There was no suitable place for livestock because the barn roof had collapsed, and the fence was sagging. But he'd fixed up the cottage, built a new barn, replaced the fencing, and had made it so attractive and industrious that the neighbors had soon given up their mistrust of the outsider.

Charl wished they were as generous toward her. But apparently generations of prejudice were harder to overcome than basic stranger anxiety.

As they approached Charl's farm, she looked at it with a critical eye. There were signs of neglect, sure, but nothing disastrous. The privy roof leaked, the garden was choked with weeds, and the orchard needed pruning. Then there was the matter of the crumbling chimney stones, but how important was a chimney really? Just because winter was coming soon was no reason to fuss.

Okay, maybe she should worry.

But the barn had been built by her grandfather and was as solid as the rocky hillside it rested against. Constructed into the mountain itself, the interior of the barn was much larger than the exterior as it extended into a large cave.

"Built to last forever," Roland had always told her with pride. And sure enough, it never seemed to age the way the rest of the farm did.

Before they entered the barn, Charl handed a

thick leather coat and gloves to Prax. They were Roland's and fit Prax well enough, though he was more muscled than Charl's brother. She donned her own gloves and coat, and Prax looked her over.

"We oughta see if Merle can fashion you a steel cap."

Charl shook her head and hefted a burlap sack that leaned against the door. "They don't like steel. They have very long memories."

Prax grunted, then opened the door to the barn and stood aside.

Light from the barn's small windows didn't reach the rafters where the hens roosted. As Charl's eyes adjusted to the dimness, she could just make out the brown, leathery shadow of a dragon.

2

STELLA

"Good morning, Stella," Charl greeted softly, knowing the dragon would have heard her long before she entered the barn. She was never quite sure just how much the dragons understood of human speech. They tended to feign ignorance most of the time, but Charl figured it was safest to assume that everything she said in a dragon's presence was being noted and remembered.

"I brought a friend with me today. You remember Praxton? He's the one who brought you that nice rabbit last time."

A glimmer of movement in the shadow showed Stella shifting. She did like rabbit immensely.

"We don't have any rabbit today, but I have two wild turkeys. I'm sure you're hungry, Stella. Can you smell them?" Charl pulled the turkeys out of the sack and threw them onto the dirt floor speckled with layers of dragon dung and dirty straw.

Stella's head emerged from under a wing. She stretched her neck to look down at the turkeys. Her large green eyes looked hungry and suspicious.

"Your sisters have already eaten," Charl said. "This is just for you. You don't even have to share."

Stella opened her mouth and coughed out a rasping sound. It was a remembered behavior from long ago before she lost her fire glands. If she'd still had them, Charl and Prax would have been roasted on the spot.

"Now Stella," Charl scolded firmly. "That's not very polite. You're just cranky because you haven't eaten all week. You'll feel a lot better if you do."

Prax moved slowly toward the wall where several long lassos and prodding spears hung. "You're a smart girl, Stella. You know what's coming, don't you? Just come down now, and we won't have to do this." He lifted a lasso and uncoiled it, testing the weight.

Stella straightened and flapped her wings in a warning. They spanned half the width of the barn, all pink on the underside. Charl strained to see how many eggs were in the nest, but it was difficult to tell from below.

"I think she's got two eggs," she murmured to Prax. "You ready?"

He nodded.

Charl grabbed a spear from the wall and threw it at Stella without even bothering to aim. While Stella coughed again and batted it away, Charl grabbed another and brandished it.

"Get down from there, you cranky old biddy," Charl growled.

Stella drew herself up to her full height and screeched. It was an angry cry that raised the hairs on the back of Charl's neck. Next to her, Prax cringed. But Charl had known that sound her whole life and didn't miss a beat.

She stepped forward and used the spear to poke at Stella's talons gripping the beam. The spear wasn't sharp enough to do any real harm. It would kill a man easily enough, but was no more than an annoyance on dragon hide.

"Get down, I said!"

Stella flexed her talons in warning. They were long and sharp enough to skewer a wild boar. Charl jabbed again, breathing heavily in the cool morning air.

Stella flexed again and shifted her weight.

"Get ready," Charl grunted at Prax as she jabbed one last time. Sure enough, Stella screeched and soared down from the rafter straight toward Charl. Charl raised the spear in warning, and Prax threw the lasso. His aim was true—mostly—and he snared Stella's snout. If he'd been a true dragon handler he could have gotten it around her neck, but the snout would work well enough.

Stella yanked back as Prax pulled, tightening the noose around her snout.

"Pull her to the ground!" Charl shouted over Stella's angry cries. Her wings flapped desperately and stirred up dust and straw, choking Charl's mouth and nose.

Prax wrestled with the rope, struggling to bring her head down. Charl edged closer, careful of the flexing talons, and poked Stella's massive chest with the spear. It took all her strength to strike the thick hide, and sweat trickled down her back.

"Down!" she bellowed at Stella. Stella shrieked back. But Prax was strong, and little by little, her head bowed to the earth. At last, she folded her wings in on herself and lay still.

"Hang on to her," Charl ordered Prax. Slowly, she approached the dragon. Stella stared at her with one glassy eye as large as a cereal bowl, and behind her anger Charl thought she saw grief. "I'm sorry you can't have your babies," Charl said more kindly, "but they wouldn't hatch anyway, Stella. You would just starve yourself to death waiting. Now, go and join your sisters. You need to get your strength back."

She reached out and rubbed her hand along Stella's head next to the spiny ridge that ran down the center of her skull. She wasn't sure if Stella could feel her hand through the thick hide, but she knew that she was smart enough to understand the gesture. She'd had generations of experience watching humans interact.

Stella blinked and cast her eye to the floor, searching for the turkeys.

"Good girl." Charl sighed with relief. "Let's take her to the cave."

With Prax tugging on the rope and Charl prodding her hindquarters, they managed to get Stella to walk to the back of the barn where it transitioned into a spacious natural cavern. Charl never set foot in there if she could help it. Roland had taught her that the dragons needed to have a space that reminded them of the days before humans in order to be content with their domesticity. It was dark and smelled even worse of dragons than the barn did.

Charl tossed the turkeys into the mouth of the cave and then carefully removed the lasso around Stella's snout. If she'd wanted to, Stella could have taken off her arm with one snap of that giant jaw. But Stella's was a mild-mannered breed, and she allowed Charl to get close with no more than a soft snort.

As soon as Charl stepped away, Stella rushed into the cave, snatching up both turkeys at the same time.

"Quick, the doors."

Together, Prax and Charl closed the large double doors that separated the cave from the roosting barn. Charl sighed, and Prax wiped his brow with his sleeve.

"Wow," he said. "And I thought mules were stubborn creatures."

"Poor Stella. Dragons are so intelligent, but when they brood, it's like they lose their minds. She'll want to give me a thrashing tonight when she comes back to roost and finds her eggs gone."

Prax looked up at the rafters overhead. "Yeeeah... do you still need help? Because I probably oughta tell you that I don't do well with heights. Call me a coward, but it's really best if I stay on the ground."

Charl laughed. "You just wrestled an adult female dragon trying to protect her eggs. I'm not going to call you a coward. But don't worry, I can manage. If you'll grab the wheelbarrow and pick them up as they drop, that would be great."

Charl hadn't been able to gather eggs for two weeks—it was far too dangerous to gather them with a dragon watching and Stella had refused to leave her nest—so now she checked each one of the nests. A tall ladder got her to the rafters, and she walked along the beams to each nest, checking for eggs and tossing any she found to the floor. In addition to Stella's two eggs, there were two more waiting in other nests. Each egg was about the size of her large iron cooking pot, but harder than any pottery or glass. Dropping them was more damaging to the dirt floor than to the eggs themselves.

As Prax gathered the eggs into the wheelbarrow, Charl swung down from the rafters and dropped to the ground below. She rubbed her hands on her trousers and grinned. "Four eggs. That'll almost be enough to let me eat next month. Thank you, Prax. That was much easier than last time."

Prax looked at the shining shells, their pearly gold surfaces faintly reflecting the light. "It still seems like an insane way of surviving."

Charl shrugged and tried to keep her voice light, but Prax's words pained her. They were too near the gossip and rumors that she'd grown up with. "I love it. They're beautiful, really. And a lot safer than you think. Never docile, of course, but only aggressive for a reason. You won't find a more intelligent creature alive."

Prax shook his head and gestured toward the eggs. "What do you want me to do with these?"

"I have a crate in the wagon. Do you mind? I'll take these to Merle tomorrow."

While Prax pushed the wheelbarrow out of the barn, Charl gathered up the dropped spears and rope. She'd have to do something nice to thank him. Facing down a broody dragon had been hard enough for the two of them. Had she been alone...well, he had saved her from some serious sore muscles if not a fresh scar or two.

As Charl removed her leather coat and gloves, a faint tapping sound carried through the stillness of the barn. She paused, looking up at the rafters for a bird or squirrel that might have made the noise. It sounded again, and something drew her closer. All was still overhead, but she knew what she heard. Faint, but insistent. It almost sounded like...

No. No, it couldn't be.

Dread crept around the edges of her stomach, and Charl grabbed the ladder, resting it against the rafter nearest Stella's nest. It was impossible.

But she climbed the ladder anyway. She had to be sure.

She reached Stella's nest and looked inside. It was empty. Of course it was empty. She was just imagining things.

Except the tapping continued, and from this

vantage point she confirmed that there weren't any birds or rodents up in the rafters making the noise.

Then Charl had an idea. She reached into the nest, among the straw and chicken feathers and bones of small rodents. Carefully, she pulled apart the top layer. Dust rose from the straw and filled her nose. She felt it before she saw it. In the shadows, beneath the coarse layers of nest, her fingers brushed something smooth and hard as polished stone.

"Stella, you clever girl," Charl whispered, even as her heart sank. How long had this egg been hidden?

She cleared away the nest until she clearly saw a crack emanating from the top of the egg. Impossible. It was one thing for Stella to hide an egg, but there was no way it could have been fertilized. Charl didn't have any male dragons. They were nearly extinct, and only a licensed breeder was allowed to keep them. To breed a dragon illegally would cause her to lose her dragons and her farm, and probably get her thrown in prison.

And yet, as Charl watched, the tapping sounded again, and the crack grew.

She had to do something. She didn't know anything about how to handle a dragon hatchling. Maybe she could hide it in the cave. She cringed at that thought. Stella's sisters would probably attack the newcomer, ensuring its death. But she couldn't keep it. And she certainly couldn't release it to the wild. All dragon farmers were catalogued. If a new dragon was discovered in the area, there was only one person who would be suspected. Charl would lose everything.

Charl hefted the egg out of the nest and awkwardly carried it down the ladder. She didn't want to risk dropping it and letting the hatchling out before she decided what to do with it. Better if she never had to see the creature.

And then—because Charl had the luck of a flame sprite trapped in a rain barrel—just as she reached the bottom of the ladder, the barn door opened.

She'd forgotten about Prax.

"What's up, Charl?" he asked. "Did you find another one?"

Panic choked her words before they could leave her throat. In the silence, the distinct tapping sounded again.

Prax frowned and looked closer at the egg she was holding. Then his face paled.

"I didn't know it was here, I swear it," Charl whispered. "Stella must have hidden it the last time she was broody, saving it this whole time."

Prax staggered back until he hit the door. "No way..."

But just at that moment, the egg shook in her arms and fell to the floor. The shell near the crack fell away, exposing a gap several inches wide. And through the gap pushed the unmistakable snout of a dragon.

3
CHANGE OF PLANS

Charl froze. Conflicting emotions swirled in her stomach. Horror and fascination at what she was seeing. Panic that Prax was there. Relief that she wasn't alone. She glanced up at him and saw the same mixture of fear and excitement on his face.

"What do we do?" he whispered.

Only part of the hatchling's mouth could fit through the opening. It opened its jaws and let out a squeak. In that moment Charl knew that she couldn't just abandon it to die in the cave.

"Go, Prax," she said firmly, looking him in the eye. "I'm sorry to involve you in this. Go home. Please."

"And just leave you to deal with this alone? No way."

Prax moved closer, and Charl stepped around the egg to stop him.

"It's fine. I'll manage. Please, Prax. I know it's not

fair to ask you to forget what you've seen, but if you can please keep it to yourself, I would be grateful."

Prax looked back and forth between Charl and the squeaking egg at her feet. His brown eyes had a spark of humor in them. "Charlotte, do you really think I'm the sort to go to the Regs over something like this? Not on your life. The last thing we need is the whole Magic Regulation Squad swarming all over Ambrey."

"Are you sure? If something goes wrong, I don't want to get you mixed up in it."Charl felt a loosening of the anxious knot in her stomach.

The hatchling continued to squeak behind her.

"Hey little guy," Prax said in a gentle voice, stepping around Charl and crouching down. He reached out and touched the wet snout, then pulled his hand away covered in slime. "Ugh." He wiped his hand on his trousers.

Emboldened by his reassurance that he wouldn't report her, Charl gave herself permission to indulge the awe she felt watching the gray scaly mouth probing the open air. She rubbed her hand along the snout, carefully noting the ridged eye tooth on top that it had used to break through the egg. Dozens of small teeth lined the inside of the jaw, but they were no bigger than a dog's tooth.

"It could be a girl, you know," Charl said hopefully. If it was a girl, it would be easier to incorporate her into the brood. Still risky, but possible. But if it were a male, that would bring nothing but trouble.

Prax didn't answer. He was running his hands

along the egg. "Do you know how long it takes to hatch?"

Charl shrugged. "It might be in my father's book. Do you mind sitting with it while I check?"

Of course he didn't mind. He was enamored.

Charl slipped carefully out of the barn and blinked in the bright sunlight. The sun had risen above the trees in the hollow, and the contrast to the dark barn made her pause momentarily to get her bearings. She ran to the cottage, hoping the dragon wouldn't hatch while she was gone. She left the door swinging on its hinges in her haste, letting daylight flood the kitchen where she ransacked the shelves above the fireplace for her family's books about dragons. In the early days after Roland left, she had studied them so thoroughly she practically had them memorized. Now they were covered in dust and cobwebs.

A Historia of Fyrdracan ond their Feonds was older than the farm itself, passed down from Charl's great-great-great-grandmother Meirdan. She'd been a scholar of some renown until publishing *A History of Dragons and their Enemies* had caused her to be thrown out of academic circles for her sympathetic view of what was considered, at the time, to be humankind's greatest threat to survival. In those days, dragons had wreaked havoc on the land, destroying villages effortlessly and ravaging whole cities unchecked. But as armor and weapons improved, humankind fought back, until after only a few generations it was the dragons who were struggling to survive. Meirdan's work—although not widely accepted at the time—had marked an important shift in advocating for the creatures' survival in a way that would allow the enemies to exist together.

Charl ran her hand lovingly over the tome, brushing off the accumulated dust from the smooth hide. She had read it often as a young girl, wishing she could have seen dragons in their wild, majestic state. Now, however, she sat it aside in favor of the newer *The Care and Keeping of Dragons*. This was a journal kept by her father over the span of about twenty years, from the time that he had assumed ownership of the farm. She flipped through the familiar pages, searching for something that would help her know how to care for the hatchling.

What was she thinking? She shouldn't be trying to care for the hatchling. If she had any sense she would dispose of it.

Instead, she searched.

The journal was written by a farmer and meant for his farmer descendants. Her father hadn't known anything about breeding or raising hatchlings. But in the very back, where her father had listed some magical considerations, Charl found something useful.

Dragon Eggs

　　The shell of a dragon egg is uncommonly hard. This is to protect the hatchling from the weight of its mother for the six months required to incubate before hatching. It is said that mother dragons will gently crush the egg with their jaws in an effort to assist the hatching process. (Today, breeders perform that labor to ensure the safety of each precious hatchling.)

Due to the hard nature of the shell, special tools are required to crack open the shell and retrieve the unfertilized embryo for use in harvesting its magical properties. Ideally this will be done by an alchemist trained in sorcersmithing. In rural areas, a common blacksmith can perform the task, although some of the rarer properties will be lost.

"Well, that was less than helpful, Papa," Charl muttered. "And just how do breeders crush the eggs?"

She fought down the familiar feeling of self-doubt that always crept into her mind when she realized how very unprepared she was to be in charge of the whole farm. Roland had disappeared nine months earlier without any warning. Charl just woke up one morning and he was gone. No note. His best boots and coat still by the back door. When he hadn't returned by nightfall, she had asked about him in the village, but people had looked at her askance and abruptly ended the conversation. The butcher had even responded with a smug, "Well, you never can tell about you lot, can you?"

Charl had stopped asking.

Praxton was the only one who had seemed sympathetic. He'd sat with her through the dark evenings of late winter, trying to puzzle out what had happened to her brother. Helping her think of things he'd said or done in recent days that might explain where he'd gone. Unusual people or places he'd visited. But Charl couldn't think of anything different in the days and weeks leading up to his disappearance. Their lives were simple and repetitive, each day stretching into the next.

Prax had helped her search the entire property and even offered to go into the cave, but the dragons had pitched a fit about that. They'd only made it a few feet past the opening before Iris and Marin had dropped in front of them, twitching their wings in a warning. Charl didn't know if it was only Prax they objected to or if she wasn't welcome either, but either way, she hadn't returned.

And neither had Roland.

Charl closed the book and returned to the barn deep in thought. Praxton sat on a stool next to the dragon egg. The hatchling hadn't broken any more of the shell since she'd left. It squeaked desperately, its little snout thrust through the hole.

"I know; it's all right," Prax murmured soothingly. "We'll get you out of there, I promise."

"That's going to be tricky," Charl said, crouching down before the egg. "Merle is the only person I can think of to ask for help, but I don't know if I can trust him."

Prax didn't respond right away.

"He has the tools. And he's always been nice to me. But what if he goes to the Regs?"

Prax rubbed his hand along the rim of the broken eggshell. "What if I try? I could ask Merle to borrow some tools and you could describe what I need. It would be less suspicious than if you go."

Charl turned this over in her mind. "But I don't even know what I'd need."

"Neither does Merle. Has he ever hatched a dragon before?"

Charl pursed her lips. Prax had a point. "Okay, let's think this through. What would mimic an adult dragon's jaws? A vise of some kind?"

"Maybe. But I doubt Merle has a vise this big. What does he normally use to break the shells?"

"Chisels. A sledgehammer. But I don't think he could do it without hurting the hatchling. He's not very delicate."

"Well, he *is* a blacksmith."

Charl rubbed at her eyes in frustration. "I can't believe this is happening. If Roland were here, he would know what to do." She looked around the barn desperately. An old door sat against one wall. Not just any door, this one had stood in the cave entrance and was almost twenty feet tall. It was weathered and worn but still solid. Not far away was the trap door that covered the small cellar where sacks of corn were stored to get the dragons through the winter when small game was scarce.

An idea started to take root, and she looked at Prax. "Okay, there might be something we could try. We're going to need your mules."

4
HATCHLING

While Prax went home to get his mules and wagon, Charl went on a hunt for a small boulder similar in size to the dragon egg. Her idea would only work if the rock was just smaller than the egg itself. Using her arms as a measure, she found one embedded in the riverbed that looked to be about right. By the time she dug it up, her hands and feet were filthy and her stomach was complaining from being neglected all day. But food would have to wait.

She heaved the rock into her arms, straining her back and legs. It was heavier than it looked. She had to set it down and rest several times before she got back to the house, careful not to drop it on her toes. By the time she got to the yard, her hair was damp with sweat. Shedding her coat and hat, she went to the barn for the egg. It was a lot lighter than the boulder and gleamed like a jewel next to the rough gray rock. A jewel that chirruped and squeaked.

Charl needed Prax's help to move the massive door, and when they laid it with one end on the egg, it formed a large, low ramp. She was pleased to see that the boulder sat just a couple of inches lower than the egg. Just right.

She hoped.

Loading the sacks of corn into the wagon bed was another sweaty chore, but with Prax's help it went faster. They worked mostly in silence, both sobered by the reality of bringing the egg outside. Charl rarely got visitors, but it would fit her poor luck to get one today, of all days, while she was in the middle of trying to hatch an illegal dragon.

"You think this will be enough?" Prax asked as he dropped the last sack of grain into the wagon.

Charl mentally reviewed her calculations. "That wagon should weigh more than an adult female. Whether it's enough or not..." She shrugged.

With the loaded wagon in position, Prax backed the mules up to the low side of the door and hitched them to the wagon. Carefully, he urged them forward on either side of the door, pulling the wagon onto the ramp.

Charl barely breathed. The mules strained and the wagon creaked as it slowly inched forward. She kept an eye on the trace chains and the door. If they held, and if the weight was enough to crack the egg, and if the boulder was the right size, the hatchling shouldn't be crushed by the weight of the wagon.

But that was a lot of *ifs*.

As both front wheels turned fully onto the door,

a loud splintering sound made Charl's heart leap into her throat. She looked at Prax and saw the same panic on his face.

"Hold, hold," he said to the mules.

The wagon teetered, rocking slightly. Charl peered at the door but couldn't see any obvious crack.

"Keep going," she instructed breathlessly.

She knelt to watch from below as the wagon ascended a few more inches. The door creaked menacingly, and Charl cried out excitedly, "It's working! The egg, it's—"

With a terrific crack, the door split and the wagon slid toward Charl. Prax yelled and yanked on the team. Charl yelped and scrambled out of the way of the tipping wagon, knees bruising against the hard ground. When all was still, she got to her feet, heart pounding.

Somehow the wagon had stayed upright, slanted with one wheel on the ground and the other still on the door. But the door was a splintered mess. With shaking hands, Prax undid the traces to move the mules away. Charl gently lifted a piece of shorn wood.

An urgent chirp greeted her. Charl met Prax's eyes and grinned. In a safe pocket next to the boulder, the egg had cracked and a little dragon was pushing its way into the world.

Prax whooped and hurried to join her, carefully moving the shards of wood away from the egg.

"We did it, Charl! Look at that!"

The dragon was gray and moist with wings

tucked against its body so tightly Charl couldn't be completely sure they were even there. It moved unsteadily on its legs, and Charl was seized with a desire to name it and feed it and keep it safe.

"I can't believe it," she said, part in wonder and part in fear as she looked at her impending doom. "What am I going to do now?"

Prax knelt down before the hatchling and ran a hand along its back. "Well, I imagine he's probably pretty hungry. Aren't you, little guy?"

"It might be a girl." *Please let it be a girl.*

The hatchling opened its mouth and Prax cooed at it. "Look at those tiny teeth. You're just a harmless little thing, aren't you?"

The dragon let out a mewling cough and ignited Prax's shirt.

5
FOREST

Prax jumped, rocking backward into the dirt and slapping at his shirt. Stunned, Charl shook herself into action, grabbing her discarded coat and rushing to smother the flames. It took only seconds, but they sat together in shock after it was over, breathing heavily.

Prax's eyes were wide as they met hers, then crinkled into a pained grin.

"I guess I should have let the dragon farmer go first."

"I—" Charl began. "I'm so sorry, Prax."

"Don't be. It was my own fault. I forgot they aren't born fireless."

"Are you badly burned?" Charl carefully removed the coat and inspected his red skin, already blistering in places. "You're lucky. If it were much older, we wouldn't have been able to smother the flames so easily."

Prax winced as he leaned forward and inspected

the burns himself. "No harm done. I probably won't even have a scar when it's healed. What's the point of a dragon wound if I can't even show the scar?"

"You wouldn't be able to tell anyone about it anyway," Charl protested, but she was relieved that he hadn't lost his good humor. "I'll get you some wet cloths."

By the time she returned with clean rags and a bucket of cold water, Prax was sitting on the wagon bed, watching the hatchling wander shakily around the yard. Already it was drying and its color was emerging as a deep green. When it opened its mouth to chirp, there were little bud-like teeth lining its jaws.

Praxton had removed what remained of his shirt, and Charl hesitated. She'd seen Prax working without a shirt before, but never from this close. And now she was supposed to touch him? Surely he would hear her heart galloping like a herd of centaurs. She tried to focus on something else besides the tautness of his muscles as she laid the wet cloths across his chest. It was no use, and heat rose in her cheeks like she'd swallowed a phoenix. But Prax didn't seem to notice, his thoughts clearly wandering.

"Who do you suppose the father is?"

"Hmm?" Charl's thoughts had wandered too. She shook her head to clear it, tossing her braid over her shoulder to avoid meeting his eyes. "There can't be a father. It's impossible."

Prax snorted. "No, it's impossible not to have a father."

"I mean, there's no way Stella could have mated

with any male dragon. The barn is secure. There are no male dragons in the area, very few even left in existence. The idea is laughable." Finished, Charl sat beside him on the wagon bed and watched the hatchling.

"Tell that to little Forest here."

"Forest?"

Prax shrugged. "He's the color of shadows in the understory of the forest."

"You don't know that it's a 'he.' And you shouldn't name it. If we were smart, we'd kill it and be done with it."

She felt Prax's glare and stubbornly kept her gaze fixed forward.

"You don't mean that," he insisted. "If you'd wanted him dead, you could have just let him die in the egg."

Charl sighed. "I said that's what we'd do if we were smart. I didn't say *I* was smart."

"Well, then. What should we do with him?"

"*We?* Are you a dragon farmer now?"

"I figure you have two options. Give him to his mother—"

"I wouldn't dare. If she's that mean when she's brooding, I'd hate to see what she's like protecting her young."

Prax smiled as if he'd expected this. "Then let me take him home."

Charl looked at him in disbelief. His light brown eyes were bright with mischief. What had happened to the sensible neighbor who had made his farm prosper through hard work and frugality?

"Are you crazy? You don't know the first thing about caring for a dragon hatchling."

"Do you?"

"Well, no, but I can learn."

"So can I."

"Don't be an idiot. You would risk everything for this?"

The hatchling was poking through the shredded wood of the door. It made a hissing sound and fire streamed out of its mouth and licked the debris.

"Oh for crying out—" Charl grabbed the bucket of water and doused the flaming door. "I can't leave you alone for one minute."

Prax laughed. "I like him. Let me take him home. That will keep him far away from Stella. There's an old dugout cellar behind my house. No wood anywhere. Nothing to catch fire. I'll keep him in there. What do you think he eats?"

Charl looked at Prax, considering, until she remembered he wasn't wearing a shirt and turned her gaze to the hatchling instead. She didn't know what to do with him any more than Prax did, and she already had her hands full with the other dragons.

"Let me get my book," she conceded. "But the second you think he's too much for you—or you're worried about being discovered—you bring him straight back. Might as well only risk one of our necks. If I go to prison, it won't do me any good for you to go with me."

Prax grinned. "Did you hear that?"

"What?"

"You called him 'he.'"

Charl growled as she headed toward the house to consult her book—not the journal of her father this time, but the older encyclopedia by Meirdan. She hastily scribbled down a few notes about hatchlings and a recipe for burn salve. Then she grabbed one of Roland's old shirts for good measure before taking it all out to Prax.

6

DRAGON OIL

Charl watched Prax until the wagon disappeared up the hill and around the bend. She'd loaned him a canvas tarp to cover the bed of the wagon, but she could still hear the dragon's squeaks until he reached the end of her lane. Once they were out of sight, she waited for a sense of relief to come, but she still felt only a heavy weight. Instead of just worrying about herself, now she had to worry about Praxton too.

He'll be fine. He's smart. He thought of muzzling the hatchling so it doesn't burn down the wagon, didn't he? Just be grateful you don't have to worry about the little beast right now.

For a moment, Charl allowed herself to marvel that Prax was willing to risk so much to help her. But then she realized it was probably just his inherent sense of adventure, not anything to do with her. He seemed genuinely excited about caring for the dragon.

Don't read too much into it, a part of her warned.

By now the sun was at its zenith. Charl had planned on taking the eggs to the blacksmith for harvesting, but the excitement of the morning had left her jittery and she wasn't sure she could be around the villagers without raising suspicion. Instead, she tended to her other chores and stayed busy enough that she forgot to fret about her Stella problem.

That is, until the sun dropped toward the horizon, setting the treetops on the hill behind the barn ablaze with light. She looked up from the garden where she was digging potatoes and wiped her damp forehead with a dirty arm.

"Ah, dirty fangs," she swore, realizing it was time to bring the dragons in to roost.

But there was nothing for it. Wishing Roland was there, she put on her gear and entered the barn. A thumping beyond the great cave doors told her they were waiting. She paused at the doors, checking to ensure her path to the exit on the other side of the barn was clear.

As soon as Charl opened the doors, Stella rushed into the barn, her brown hide almost black in the low light. The air from her wings beat against Charl as she took to the air. Marin and Iris were close behind, and as soon as the last tail had cleared the door, Charl slid it shut and bolted for the outside door.

She wasn't fast enough.

Stella had already reached her nest and discovered the theft. She screamed in fury, her wings batting the air and her neck stretched high to the rafters. Then she dove for Charl.

Charl was still too far from the door. She reached for the closest weapon she could find—a wooden spear—and rounded on Stella.

"Stay back!" she shouted, but her voice trembled.

Stella wasn't just cranky anymore. She was furious. She shrieked a ghastly sound, lips curled back and teeth bared. Her jaws snapped the end of the spear and it reverberated so hard in Charl's hands that she dropped it.

Stella roared, hot spittle flying into Charl's face. Desperately, Charl tried to remember what she'd been taught about subduing an unruly dragon. But these dragons had never been unruly. They were usually so easy to manage, the most mild-mannered of the domesticated breeds.

Staring her down to assert dominance, Charl drew her dagger and tried not to blink. "I don't want to hurt you, Stella. And you don't want to hurt me. Go back to your nest. Go!"

Stella snarled but stopped moving forward.

"I said go!" Charl's eyes burned with the effort of not blinking. She tried to keep her voice deep and commanding, but it was nothing like Roland's deep bellow.

Out of the corner of her eye, she saw movement and realized that Marin had jumped down behind Stella. There was no way Charl could face down two dragons at once.

This is it, she thought, imagining the two of them

tearing her to pieces. She adjusted the grip of her dagger in her sweaty palm. She'd go for the nostril first, eyes if she could reach them. When Prax found her eviscerated body later, she hoped it would be clear that she'd put up a noble fight.

But Marin nipped at Stella's flank, distracting her. Stella turned and hissed, and Marin hissed back. Marin arched her wings and snorted threateningly. Charl took a cautious step toward the door as the two female dragons groused at each other, careful not to attract attention.

When she was almost to the door, she turned and ran the last few steps. Behind her, Stella rasped a submissive cry. She took to the air, but just as Charl reached for the handle, the dragon lashed out with one talon in a parting shot.

Heat seared through Charl's back as she staggered out into the fading light of dusk. Blinded by pain, she fumbled with the latch, closing the door by feel rather than sight. Through the haze, she reached around to her back and felt shredded leather, sticky and wet.

Curse you, Stella. And curse you, Roland. If you hadn't left me, I wouldn't be facing these dragons alone.

She had to stop the bleeding. She had to make a poultice. She had to clean the wound of any dragon oil. But she could barely stagger to the well. She leaned against it, trying to muster the strength to draw water.

"Charl! Charl, what happened?"

Prax's voice made her want to weep with relief. She looked up and could just make out a shape running up the lane. This was hardly the noble fight she'd imagined. Was her vision dim because it was almost night? Or did it just seem that way because she was struggling to stay conscious?

"It's dragon oil. It must be. I can't...think straight."

Soon he was at her side, gasping at the sight of the wound.

"Tell me what to do," he commanded, but his voice was higher than usual.

"Clean it. Stop the bleeding. Make a poultice. It's all in the book."

Arms were lifting her awkwardly and carrying her to the house, muddy boots and all. She thought she should be embarrassed but decided there would be time for that later.

Prax laid her face down on Roland's bed, kicking aside the dirty washing piled there. She'd have to be embarrassed about that later, too. Pain turned her vision dark around the edges. She tried to blink it away, but it wouldn't clear.

"I've got the book. What do I do, Charl?"

She tried to muster the will to sit up and thumb through her father's journal. She knew right where to go for treating injuries, but just the thought of sitting upright was too much. Instead, she closed her eyes and surrendered to the darkness.

7
TOUCH

When Charl woke, her first sensation was of being uncomfortably warm. Sweat clung to her, and she tried to shrug off the quilt. Immediately, pain erupted between her shoulder blades, and a hand was there with a soothing voice.

"Don't move. It's all right. Just lay still."

"Hot," Charl murmured, her mouth like wool.

"Let me help."

A cool wet rag pressed against her face, and she sighed. Firelight flickered behind her eyelids, and she relaxed into the straw mattress, letting Roland tend to her as she drifted back toward sleep.

A mournful yowl drifted eerily on the night air. Stella. Stella was still angry with her. Stella had struck her, and she'd been hurt. Someone had come—

Not Roland.

Praxton.

Charl's eyes flew open. She tensed like a fawn catching the scent of a panther.

Prax sat near her holding the wet rag. Meirdan's book lay open on his lap.

"Hey Charlotte," he said quietly.

Charl tried to sit up and gasped, realizing two uncomfortable truths very quickly. First, as soon as she moved, searing pain shot through her back. Second, she wasn't wearing a shirt.

Mortified, her face flooded with heat.

"It's all right," Prax said, jumping to help. "Lay down. Best if you don't have any quick movements."

Charl lay on her side, pulling the quilt up to her chin. The pain eased slightly once her back was relaxed.

"This is the worst moment of my life," she moaned. "I wish you'd just left me there to die in the dirt."

Prax chuckled softly. "No, you don't. You told me where to find the antidote for the dragon oil, remember?"

"I remember the burning. Then you were there." She squinted at him. "Why did you come back?"

"You'd said Stella would be a challenge when she saw what you'd done. I thought you might need some help. Not that it matters, since I was too late."

Charl tried to shake her head. "Not your fault. I'm just no good at this. Without Roland, I'm hopeless. Stella could have killed me."

"She could have killed Roland just as easily," Prax said practically.

"Maybe I should do what you said," Charl said, tears forming at the corners of her eyes. "Maybe I should just give up and sell them all and...and...I don't know what I'd do." She knew it was probably just the lingering effects of the dragon oil pulling on her emotions, but all the months of loneliness pressed against her defenses, and she felt as if a great dam inside her was cracking.

Prax stepped away as she buried her face in the quilt, but he returned a moment later with a cup of cool water.

"Drink this. Now's not the time to be making any decisions. You're a great dragon farmer. It's in your blood. And you love it, I know you do. These last few months have been hard, but you'll enjoy it again. You're a natural."

The water soothed Charl's parched throat, and she realized how thirsty she was. Prax had to fill it two more times before she was satisfied. When she was finished, she felt like the dam had sealed up again.

"Thank you for helping me, Prax," she said, calmer now. She peered around his shoulder, expecting to see her kitchen ransacked, but everything looked neat and tidy. "You found everything you needed?"

"There were a few things mislabeled, and I had to substitute Eye of Mae for the Blushield."

Charl nodded. She knew where the Blushield was, but of course he wouldn't know her haphazard system. "Thank you. I don't know how I'll ever repay you."

Prax leaned back in his chair, its wooden legs creaking. "I hope you don't think I'm the kind of man who thinks every kindness puts you in my debt."

"Doesn't it?"

"You might not think so after you get a look at that scar. Sorry, my sewing skills are a little rusty."

Charl grimaced. "Just one more trophy to add to the collection, I guess." Oh well. It's not as if she were some great beauty to begin with. She knew her jaw was a little too narrow and her eyes had that funny shape all members of her family shared. What did it matter if she were scarred and maimed as well? She was never going to attract the kind of man who valued beauty.

"Let me take a look at it," Prax offered, "make sure you didn't start bleeding again moving around."

Charl felt herself blushing as he lifted the quilt and inspected the light wrappings. They tugged when he pulled them, catching on the stitching.

"Um...ouch?" She bit her lip.

"Sorry, I don't mean to be clumsy. It looks all right. I'll put more salve on in the morning, but for now you should rest."

Charl watched the shadows from the firelight flicker across the opposite wall. She did feel bone weary, but there was one thing that still bothered her. "We haven't talked about the fact that you saw me with my shirt off."

Now it was Prax's turn to blush. "Charl, I would never...I did have to take off your shirt, but I swear I didn't take advantage in any way. Please don't think—"

"It's all right." Charl yawned. "I just wanted to make sure you feel as uncomfortable about it as I do."

She closed her eyes, and Prax's chair squeaked as he shifted. "Honestly, I didn't have time to feel anything but panicked. I was so worried about you, Charl."

He laid a tentative hand on her head, stroking her hair behind her ear. His touch was soothing, and she closed her eyes, feeling a little lightening of the heavy weight she'd carried all day. Somehow, his touch felt nicer than Roland's in a way she didn't want to admit.

Her mind wandered to thoughts of her brother, and she pictured his face, his eyes dark under heavy brows. As she drifted to sleep, the eyes changed, their shape becoming more pronounced, the brows more defined. They were a woman's eyes, shaped like Charl's, but flecked with gold. The woman's skin had an almost golden sheen to it as well, darker than Charl's as if she spent her days under a hot sun. Her hair was braided around her head in a thick crown, and she wore earrings that glinted like firelight. She looked at Charl and smiled warmly before fading into oblivion.

8

MEIRDAN'S STORY

For four days, Charl lay in bed, sleeping off the effects of the dragon oil and trying to get her strength back.

For four days, Prax mended fences, relaid thatch, harvested her garden, and chopped firewood.

For four days, Stella whined from the barn, her angry shrieks dwindling to a melancholy moan.

Charl forbade Prax from entering the barn. "They'll be fine for a few days without food. In the wild they go a lot longer than that."

He didn't force the issue.

"Here, have some tea." He propped her up, being careful not to touch her back, and held out a cup of the bland hendel tea she'd been taking for pain. "I've been studying your dragon books. There's not a lot related to hatchlings."

Charl grimaced as she swallowed the tepid tea. "Our dragons were grown adults two generations ago. I guess no one in my family thought to pass the knowledge on. They just assumed our dragons would live forever, I guess." Then a thought occurred to her. "How are you reading Meirdan's book? I can barely decipher it myself."

"It's not the first time I've read old script, but I admit it's taking longer than I expected. You oughta find a scribe willing to copy it out fresh, with updated spellings and a clearer hand. I'd hate for her words to get lost to time."

"She's remarkable, isn't she? I can't imagine the courage it took to go against everyone she knew and loved in order to save the dragons. She must have been fierce."

"Are the stories true that she could talk to dragons?"

Charl yawned. "She never comes right out and says so. Maybe it was an exaggeration, a way her enemies tried to turn people against her. Or maybe she started the rumors herself as a way of earning respect. I don't know, but when I was younger I believed the folklore and tried to see if I could get our dragons to talk to me by staring them down. But they couldn't care less. When my mother found out what I was doing, she explained that our dragons weren't like the wild ones. To make eye contact with dragons in the wild—the old greats that Meirdan cared for— would have meant certain death. If Meirdan could speak to dragons, the skill was lost with the last of the great dragons. Part of the price of domestication."

"You must be proud of that heritage, to be a direct descendant of Meirdan the Protector."

Charl finished off the tumbler and settled back against the pillow. "I am. I know we're not changing the world in the same way Meirdan did, but at least we're proving that we can exist together."

"With only a few scars to show for it," Prax added with a teasing smile. "Get some rest. I'll be outside if you need me."

The tea was making her sleepy again, and she closed her eyes, thinking of all she should have said. She should have apologized to Prax that he was neglecting his own farm to care for hers. She should have felt embarrassed that even when healthy she couldn't accomplish as much in a day as he did. But as she drifted off to sleep against the familiar sound of splitting wood, she felt comforted. It reminded her of days when the farm had prospered under Roland's care. Or when her parents were alive and shouldered the greatest burdens themselves. What would they have done about Forest? If only she could ask.

The next time Charl awoke, all was quiet and still. Prax must have gone home for the night.

Meirdan's book lay on the short table next to the bed. She reached for the heavy book and held it on her lap, easing up into a sitting position. She gently rubbed the smooth leather as she might stroke a kitten or a child. The light coming in through the window was meager, but it would be enough to read for a little while.

She opened the book to the introduction and read. Meirdan's story was like that of an old friend; she'd read it so many times in her youth.

The tale is told of the first day dragons appeared in the skies of this land, passed down among my people for seven generations. The wind was filled with the beating of wings and the scream of hell as the great beasts dropped out of the sky and pierced livestock, man, woman, and child alike, carrying them away until their cries for deliverance could only be heard echoing in the minds of those who loved them. Fire swept away villages made of wood and straw, leaving behind only ash and sorrow. Our ancestors gathered in larger cities behind stone walls, but even they could not protect against creatures who claimed the sky.

Sometimes the dragons didn't return for years at a time, but our ancestors never forgot their power to destroy. They made long spears and arrows that flew true and protected themselves with the strongest steel. The bravest of all didn't wait for the dragons to return. They hunted for them instead.

When I came into this world, only three dragons had been seen in this land during my parents' lifetime. As a daughter of the court, it was my privilege to learn the stories, hear the tales told by slayers who returned from the wilds of the north with trophies of dragon hide and claw, and even join my father and mother on a hunt of their own.

It was on such a hunt that I first met a live dragon, on the banks of a river cascading over a cliff so high one of our party nearly swooned when he looked over the edge. The slayer suspected that a Reshkath had made its den somewhere in the hill-

side nearby where great trees grew despite the massive rocks breaking through the earth, their snarling roots exposed where the dirt had washed away. Curtains of moss and heavy vines covered nooks and crevices, and it was these we set about searching, to see if one looked like it opened into a cave deep enough to house a dragon.

It was my father who found the den, little more than a burrow littered with bones and scales. I wanted to see the dragon before they slew it and pushed my way to the front until my mother held me back with an arm around my shoulder.

"They are trained, and you are not," she said. "Watch and learn."

In the deep recess where daylight didn't shine, two men held torches while the slayer led my father and four other soldiers. The soldiers held spears, but the slayer had only a thick rope tied on the end of a long pole. We didn't speak. The only sound was the scrape of our boots on stone and the creak of oiled leather and whisper of steel against steel for those few like my father who wore armor. Yet the dragon was waiting for us anyway.

I know now that he must have been very old for his fire to burn so mildly. It barely reached the first soldier, who cried out and slapped at the flames scorching his heavy leather tunic. The slayer was very skilled. He tossed the rope just as the dragon breathed in to turn his attention to another. It slipped easily around his snout, and the slayer pulled it tight.

While the dragon wrestled with the rope, my father rushed in with his spear. He and the other soldiers thrust them into the beast's exposed underbelly. Two of them found their mark, and with a desperate, choked roar, the dragon staggered. His barbed tail whipped out of the shadows, and my mother screamed as it raked across my father, knocking him to the earth and leaving him sliced nearly in two. Something wet slashed across my face as the man holding the torch was flung against the wall nearest me. The torch landed near my feet and sputtered.

Cries of the wounded men were drowned out by the bellows of the dragon.

I wiped my face, and my hand came away dark with blood. Darker than the red of my hair. Dark like Father's blood leaking out onto the ground in a steady river.

"Help me hold him! Where's the light?" the slayer shouted. I couldn't tell if he was angry or afraid.

I reached for the torch at my feet and held it high.

"Meirdan!" Mother tried to pull me back, but a soldier was dragging Father out of the way. She couldn't tend to us both and so let me go.

I stepped forward shakily, trying not to look the dragon directly in the eyes, but eager to see him more clearly all the same. He was the color of wood that has been so long at sea that it floats as lightly as a newborn chick.

"Watch the tail!" the slayer cried and side-stepped it, but the man helping to hold the line didn't move fast enough.

A barb lodged in his back, and when the dragon whipped his tail back, the soldier snapped back with it, impaled on the end like a goose roasting over the fire.

Behind me came the sounds of men and women fleeing the cave, dragging their wounded with them. Only three of us remained to face the dragon. The slayer, the last soldier who now held the rope, and myself, trying to find a way to hold the torch without blinding myself to the darkness.

The dragon tried to sweep his tail at the slayer, but the barbed end moved more slowly now that it carried the weight of a man, and the slayer moved easily out of the way.

The dragon was weakening. Blood the color of pitch marred his smooth underbelly where the spears still pierced his hide.

As the sounds of battle faded, the chamber was filled with the sound of his breathing, and he wheezed as if each breath cost him more than it was worth.

The slayer and the soldier pulled the rope, wrestling the dragon's head closer to the earth until his forefeet touched the ground. The slayer seemed to notice me for the first time.

"You, girl! You're all that remained?"

I didn't know how to answer a question whose answer was so apparent.

"Lay your torch against the wall there and come hold the rope."

I obeyed. The rope was thick and coarse, and I wished for gloves, but I said none of this.

I stood behind the soldier, close enough to feel the dragon's warm breath as he bared his long teeth. They were limned with yellow, and at least two were broken clear off.

The slayer approached the head which still stood taller than his own. He raised a sword and aimed for the soft underside of the dragon's neck, where the skull connected to the sinuous spine.

The dragon jerked his head, and I stumbled forward but held the line. The slayer's sword found its mark, and the dragon let out a howl through his clenched jaw that made the hairs on the back of my neck stand up. Blood ran over the slayer's arm, and something white hung from behind the jaw. A tendon or muscle or bone, I couldn't tell.

I had seen many creatures die on the hunt, usually deer or boar that filled the forests and our bellies. But this was different.

It felt like an execution.

"It won't be long now," the slayer said, his tone triumphant as he grabbed the rope again and yanked the dragon's head all the way to the earth.

I found myself trembling and dropped the rope. At last, I looked the dragon in the eye. It was slitted like a serpent and the color of copper. There was no harm he could do me now. He watched me without blinking.

Child of destruction. Child of death.

The words slipped into my mind like a whisper. I thought of my father lying bleeding outside the cave—perhaps dead, I didn't know. If he died, the legacy he left to me was the sight of this dragon bleeding out helpless and bound. We had brought destruction. We had brought death. To the dragon as well as our own.

A dark liquid seeped out between the dragon's jaws, and the intelligence in his eyes slipped away. It was there that I determined to leave a new legacy, one that promised life to dragon and human both.

It's been almost four decades since I met my first dragon. I've met many since, and each is as unique as the last. They know me now. They call me Protector. Emissary. Even Noble One, though I've long since lost any title that should have come to me. I rejected the life I might have had to learn all I can about these ancient creatures and how we might live together in this world.

Within these pages you'll find my research. May you find it illuminating, and may you find the subject—these majestic creatures of the skies— worthy of protecting.

The room was now nearly dark, and Charl could only read the words because she'd practically memorized them. She loved this story. Not the death of the old dragon, of course, but the heroic way that it changed Meirdan. Her father did indeed die from that wound, Charl knew. Meirdan's mother allowed her to roam wild as a way of coping, never guessing that she was going out to find dragons—not to slay them in revenge, but to study and learn all she could about them.

Her legacy had been to save the dragons and create a way for dragon and human to co-exist. By comparison, Charl's legacy so far was to neglect this trust and get herself injured for her trouble. She was proving to be a poor steward indeed.

9
RESTLESS

O n the fifth day, Charl was standing at the door wrapped in a shawl when Prax came. She had managed to pull on her boots, but her stitches ached from the effort and she felt unsteady on her feet.

"The dragons are restless," she said. "I need to let them out."

Prax eyed her with a frown. "I'll do it. Should I just let them into the cave?"

"You've already done so much. I won't have you risk yourself unnecessarily. But stay close in case I need your help."

Charl wished she could stride confidently to the barn to show Prax that she had regained her strength, but her confident stride was more like a slow shuffle. She coughed in the cold morning air thick with fog. It was good to move and work her lungs a little. Lying still too long could bring a chest weakness, especially when one was already trying to heal from a nasty wound.

She hesitated in front of the door, her hand resting on the latch. She tried to tell herself she was gathering her strength, but she knew it wasn't that. It was fear that made her pulse race. Dread of what she might find when she opened that door.

I can't face her again.

Charl gripped the bolt and slid it open.

She stepped inside and immediately looked to the rafters. In the morning shadows, she could just make out the three massive creatures snuffling in their nests. They were agitated, annoyed at being left alone.

"That's what you get for throwing a tantrum," she muttered. She followed the wall to the barrel of grain in the corner. When she felt well enough, she would check her traps, but for now they would have to settle for corn.

Pushing away the thought that it was too early in the season to be using her corn stores, Charl scooped four pails into a trough. A heavy thump behind her announced that a dragon had dropped from the rafters. She turned, gripping the pail, but it would be a poor weapon if she needed to defend herself.

Marin ignored her and eagerly attacked the grain, soon followed by Stella and Iris. Charl edged around them toward the cave door, taking advantage of their distraction. In a moment, the trough was empty and they nipped at each other over the crumbs.

"Come on, girls. You've been cooped up here too

long." Charl was relieved that Stella seemed back to her normal mild disposition. She suspected she hadn't forgotten about Charl stealing her egg, but her earlier rage seemed to have passed.

Still, Charl didn't breathe a sigh of relief until after she'd closed the door behind the dragons. She'd done it. It was a small thing, but she felt a sense of triumph as she stepped back out into the morning mist. Prax was waiting for her, a frown of concern shadowing his eyes.

"Everything okay?"

"Dragons and farmer both alive and well." She managed a smile.

Prax smiled back, a small dimple appearing below his eye that made Charl feel a pleasant tingle. "It's good to see you on your feet, Charl."

"Thanks to you. I can't thank you enough for all you've done."

Prax's smile fell, and a line appeared between his brows. "I wish I could do more. I'll be honest, Charl, I'm worried about you. Your stores are awfully lean. Have you thought of how you're going to get through the winter?"

Charl felt the cold of dread in her heart even as her cheeks flushed hot. "I'll be fine. I just need to get those eggs to town while they're still potent. I'm only one person, and I don't eat much."

It was humiliating to know that Prax saw her desperate situation so clearly. But what could she do? Moaning to him about it wouldn't fix anything.

He frowned doubtfully. "You can't take those eggs in your condition. Let me do it."

She knew he was only trying to help, but it irked her. She wasn't completely helpless, after all.

"It's gotta be me. Merle would take advantage of you and you wouldn't even know it."

The cold was beginning to seep through her boots, so she headed back to the house.

Prax called after her. "And how do you think you're going to pull that cart all the way to town?"

"The same way I have for the past six months," Charl snapped back over her shoulder.

"With the skin between your shoulder blades freshly sewn shut?" He trotted to catch up to her. "Be reasonable, Charl."

Charl stopped at the door, glaring at a knot that disrupted the cascading grain of the wood. It annoyed her that he was right. "Don't you have something better to do than pestering me?"

Prax laughed at the ire in her tone. "Pestering you is what I do best. Come on, Charl. At least let me go with you. I'll bring my wagon." He climbed the steps and leaned against the door, raising his eyebrows plaintively.

"Fine. Just this once. But if you don't stop doing so much neighborly service, I'm going to have to run you off my property." She bit back a smile.

In the end, she was grateful for his offer. By the time he returned home and came back with his mule team, she had eaten and plaited her hair and put on a clean shirt. The skin on her back itched and ached simultaneously, and she knew she never would have made it very far pulling the cart alone. But larger livestock didn't tolerate living near dragons, so Charl's family had always gone without.

Which is why selling the eggs was vitally important. There would be no fresh milk, no wool, and no meat without them. If she had even a single milking goat, the prospect of a winter alone would be less daunting. But the old nanny goat had broken her tether and wandered off during a spring storm, and Charl hadn't had the means to replace her.

With the eggs loaded into the wagon, Charl crouched over the remnants of Forest's broken shell. The membrane had dried in the days she'd been sick. The shell itself was probably worth something, but how could she bring it to Merle's without explaining what had happened?

In the end, she gathered the pieces and placed them in a tin pail by the back door to deal with later.

"How is Forest doing?" Charl asked as they drove up the hill to join the road.

"Mischievous and sweet-tempered. I swear he knows me now. He doesn't breathe fire every time I open the cellar hatch."

"Makes sense. You're the one who feeds him. He's starting to trust you. But don't think you can trust him. He's still just as likely to fry you if you give him a chance. How's your burn, anyway?" Charl felt a moment of chagrin realizing that while Prax had been tending to her, he'd been dealing with his own dragon wound alone.

"It blistered up pretty good, but that salve you gave me worked wonders. Barely anything left." After a moment of silence, he added, "I wish he didn't have to be down there all alone in that hole."

"He's fine, especially if he is a 'he'. Dragons are solitary creatures, males most of all. I'd be more worried about what you're going to do with him when he outgrows the cellar." Charl wondered how long it would take until Forest could fly out of it on his own. She would need to study up on the growth and development of hatchlings.

"I don't suppose you know how to remove fire glands?"

"Sorry. I'm not a breeder."

The irony of that statement hung in the silence between them. She wasn't a breeder. And yet, Prax had a hatchling hidden at his house. He had the courtesy not to point that out.

"It's too bad, though," she added. "Fire glands are extremely valuable. They don't have much yield, but if you get enough of them you can make a candle that lasts years. Decades, even."

"I've heard of those," Prax nodded. "Never seen one myself."

"I have. My father got one once from a breeder he did business with. A long time ago. Most of the candles today are diluted so much that they only last a few years. But this was premium strength. Rumored to last generations."

Prax whistled. "That must have been worth a fortune."

Charl looked away. "That was during better times." She didn't mention that she still had the everlight candle. Her father had intended it as a dowry. But she didn't want to marry someone who only sought her hand because of a dowry, and telling Prax now felt too much like a sales pitch.

Of course, it was too valuable for everyday use. She didn't get many visitors, but a candle would be far too easy to steal. So instead, it stayed packed away, worth a king's ransom but absolutely useless to her.

"I once heard of an alchemist who could fire-proof wood," Prax said. "She rose to prominence fortifying her king's navy until an enemy captured her for their own gains. It didn't end well for her, unfortunately. I always wondered if the rumors were true."

"It's possible, I suppose. Papa talked about lots of uses when you have a proper sorcersmith and alchemist working together. But that was strictly with eggs. Some of the more valuable ancient uses require the death of the dragon. Now that dragon popula-tions are so carefully controlled, those extreme uses are very rare. It certainly wouldn't do me any good to harm my dragons, would it?"

"Of course not. It would be more useful to increase your flock than anything else."

Charl shot him a look. "If it weren't highly illegal, you mean."

The wagon crested the hill and began its descent,

jostling them both on the rutted road. Charl braced herself, leaning forward to protect her back, but the effort pulled at her stitches and she was beginning to get a headache from gritting her teeth. To distract herself from the pain, she imagined what it would be like if she didn't risk imprisonment by keeping Forest. Could she sell him? Male dragons were rare and could command an exorbitant price. If Forest was a female, could Charl train her up and add her to her brood? An increase of eggs would be a godsend.

"My father knew several breeders. I wonder if any of them would be willing to buy an illegal hatchling. Or even produce a contract for me so it looked like I bought Forest myself."

Prax shot a look at her. "You're talking about forgery? That would only make things worse for you if you were discovered."

"Maybe. I don't know. It's a moot point anyway because I wouldn't even know who to trust. Roland took over some of the correspondence after our father died, but he didn't talk to me about it much. Just said he was keeping up good will in case we were ever in a position to increase our brood. It seemed so far-fetched that I didn't concern myself with particulars."

Charl sighed heavily. If she'd known she would be managing the farm on her own someday, she would have paid more attention.

"Look!" Prax pointed to a pair of swans gliding on the river as they crossed over the stone bridge outside Ambrey. "That's good luck. Maybe you'll make a little extra today."

But Charl couldn't share his enthusiasm. This side of harvest the villagers would be watching their wallets with a wary eye toward winter. And if there was one thing she'd learned over the past two years, it was that luck rarely favored dragon-farming orphans.

10

TROUBLE IN THE VILLAGE

The sun struggled to break through the icy fog just as Charl and Prax drove into town. Ambrey was little more than a cluster of small farms that had banded together three generations back and given themselves a name. It had grown, as villages do when the babies are born healthy and thrive through childhood. Charl knew the women of Ambrey wouldn't dream of going through a pregnancy without one of Sasha's tinctures to guarantee a full nine months with a healthy baby at the end of it. But she wondered how many of the women knew the tinctures were more potent because of the distillations Sasha performed with Charl's eggs.

They passed Sasha's apothecary shop, and Charl glimpsed a face at the window before the curtain fluttered shut. Sasha frequently came to visit with Charl while she was at Merle's. Roland had never said as much, but Charl had suspected he and Sasha might have formed an attachment. It would have been a brilliant match, merging the two family businesses together. And Charl liked Sasha. She was quick-witted with an easy laugh, and if Roland hadn't disappeared, Charl would have been pleased to one day call her "sister."

But Sasha didn't appear. In fact, the road through town seemed unusually quiet.

"It isn't Sabbath, is it?" Charl asked, wondering if she'd lost track of the days in her illness.

"No," Prax murmured. "Empty like it is, though, isn't it?"

They turned onto a side street that wound a little way out of town until Merle's blacksmith shop appeared, a dark mass taking shape in the mist. A glow showed the forge was lit, and Merle's bulk shifted near it as they approached.

Charl's eyes strayed to the warm fire longingly, her hands and face icy cold from their drive.

Merle frowned as Prax helped her down from the wagon. "You're the last person I expected to see today. Thought you'd be laying low with all the Regs in town."

Charl's heart skipped a beat. "I'm here 'cause I've got a couple of eggs that need harvesting. What Regs are you talking about?"

Merle scratched at his graying beard. "You haven't heard then? Regs came into town yesterday. New ones. Asking a lot of questions about you." He gestured with a chisel before placing the end of it in the fire.

Panic surged through her heart, and she resisted

looking at Prax. "Why not just come and talk to me? I'm not hard to find."

"Oh, I'm sure they will soon enough. You haven't been doing anything you shouldn't up on that mountain, have you?"

Merle placed the hot chisel against the tip of the first egg and pounded against it with a large mallet. The reverberation shook the worktable and rang through Charl's teeth. Charl snuck a glance at Prax and saw the same worry she felt reflected in his eyes. Once the chisel cracked through the shell, Merle flipped the egg over to put a hole on the opposite end, pausing to heat the end of the chisel again. Charl moved closer to the forge, trying to warm herself in the damp chill.

Prax moved next to her and murmured softly under the sound of the ringing mallet. "It's a coincidence. Only you and I know about Forest."

"That's a pretty awful coincidence," Charl hissed. Her back ached and she dreaded the drive home, but at the same time she was anxious to leave.

With the first egg draining into a large pot, Merle started on the second. Charl wished Sasha would come. Her absence seemed portentous. The second egg didn't yield as easily, and by the time he finally broke through, cracks ran along the sides and the top was smashed in. Charl sighed. The extra airflow when it drained would further dilute the potency, but that was the hazard when using a blacksmith.

While they waited for the eggs to drain, Charl asked Merle about his family. She was grateful Prax was there to help carry the conversation because all she could think about was the Regs. Why were they asking questions about her? She was nobody. The attention wouldn't earn her the good will of the town.

"I'll pick up the shells later," Charl said, sealing the jars with their lids when the eggs were finished draining. The shells had to be dried thoroughly before being crushed into powder, a process which ordinarily took weeks but could be finished in a few days at the forge.

"I don't know, Charl." Merle scratched at his ear and folded his arms. "I don't want Regs hanging around causing trouble. I think you'd better take 'em home and dry them yourself."

Charl felt her cheeks warming and looked away from Merle, avoiding his eyes. "Of course. I understand." She lifted the first egg, which was much lighter now, and hefted it into the wagon, biting back a curse against the painful pulling of her stitches.

Prax snorted derisively, and Charl sensed him bristle beside her. "I didn't figure you for a man who'd get scared by a couple of Regs, Merle. Charl hasn't done anything wrong, and it's not illegal for you to help her."

Charl flushed hotter at his words, and she silently wished for Prax to leave it alone.

"You can't fault me for not wanting trouble," Merle replied. "Bring 'em back when they're dry and I'll grind 'em up for you. Maybe by then the Regs will be gone."

Prax nodded and reached for the other egg. "Fastest way to get rid of the Regs is to continue business as usual. You start acting like you're trying to hide something and they'll be on you like a wood sprite in late summer."

Merle grunted and turned away.

Charl didn't know what to say as they left the smithy behind. She felt like she should thank Prax for defending her, but she also guessed he wouldn't want her thanks. More than anything, she worried about the Regs and was ashamed that someone like Merle—whom her family had done business with since before she was born—would cast her aside so easily at the first sign that something was wrong.

"Sasha didn't come," she said. "Do you think she's scared of the Regs too?" The Regs couldn't have come at a worse time. If her customers stopped doing business with her, there was no way she'd have the stores she needed for winter. And judging by the thick berries forming on the wild holly off the side of the road, it was going to be a bad one.

Prax didn't answer, but his expression was dark. He stopped the mules next to Sasha's house, her neat little garden overflowing with yellowing plants and stalks black from the first frost.

"I'll bring the jars," Prax offered.

Charl shuffled to the door, pulling her shawl tighter around her. Sasha opened the door before she could knock.

"Come inside, quick," she said, barely opening the door wide enough for Charl to slip through. She smoothed her apron neatly, her deep brown skin a pleasing contrast to the cream colored fabric. "I would have thought you'd stay away for a while. Haven't you heard about the Regs? They've got a trapper with them."

Charl's stomach clenched. Why would Regs bring a trapper to Ambrey? "I've been sick. Haven't heard any news. But I've got two fresh eggs that Merle just—"

"I can't take them now," Sasha said, shaking her head before Charl could finish. "I don't know what those Regs want, and I'm not about to find out."

"But Sasha, I can't store them right. Every day they diminish in potency. I can't promise that they'll be effective if you wait."

Sasha's eyes looked pained, but her jaw was firm. "Then I'll just have to go without this batch."

Charl felt as if the air was sucked out of the room. Sasha was her most reliable customer. There were other apothecaries in Ambrey, but Charl's family had primarily worked with Sasha's. If she had to find someone else to take the eggs, it might take days or weeks. She'd be selling inferior goods on the cheap. It'd be a terrible way to start a new business relationship and wouldn't be enough to get her the supplies she needed to avoid starving through the winter.

A knock sounded at the door. Prax came in with the two jars, one in each arm. Sasha's transformation was immediate. Her eyes brightened, and she smiled brilliantly.

"Praxton! What brings you here?" She smoothed a ringlet of hair back behind her ear.

Prax smiled warmly in a way that made Charl feel like she'd swallowed sour milk.

"I've got Charl's jars here for you. Freshly drained."

Sasha's eyes widened. "Oh, how kind of you. I'm afraid I won't be needing them this time, but would you like a cup of fresh tea? I've got a pot on, and it's awfully chilly out there."

"You don't need them?" Prax glanced at Charl. His smile fell as he saw her expression. He shifted his weight under the burden of the twin jars. "I guess... I'll just go put them back then?"

"No need to rush," Sasha said sweetly, taking a jar from one arm. "Come in and have a seat. Both of you. I'll go get the tea."

Charl felt herself winding tighter than a basilisk on the kill. If she had to stay one more minute watching Sasha flirt with Prax, her stitches would snap from the tension. She grabbed the jar from Sasha. "It's fine. We need to get back. Sorry to bother you."

She pushed past Prax and out the door. Before it closed behind her she heard Sasha's cheery, "Oh, well then. Maybe another time, Praxton?"

Charl sat alone in the wagon, waiting for Prax to emerge from the cottage. The cold air bit at her cheeks, but she barely noticed. Instead, she could only think of Sasha's expression as she invited Prax inside. Sasha used to look at Roland with that hopeful look in her big dark eyes. It was Roland she saved her best smiles for. When had she transferred her affections to Prax?

It's not like they were wed, a reasonable voice in Charl's mind reminded her. *You can't expect her to wait forever to see if Roland will return, can you?* It still felt like bitter betrayal, and the childish part of her told the reasonable part of her to stuff it. She had to bite back a snide comment when Prax finally appeared.

If she were honest with herself, she had to admit it hurt worse because, of all the men she could have chosen, Sasha had her eyes on Prax. Charl knew that Prax knew his own mind and wouldn't return Sasha's affection unless it were genuine. She knew that Sasha's favor didn't necessarily change anything about Charl and Prax's friendship. But she still felt miserable as they started their rocking drive back up the mountain.

Fortunately, Prax didn't guess the nature of her dark thoughts. "I know you're worrying about the Regs, but it's probably nothing. I've seen your logbook, and your records are thorough. They're probably just doing a routine check-up on their way to Rennerton."

"Sasha says they brought a trapper."

"Oh."

The silence fell thick between them.

As they passed the road to Prax's house, he grumbled, "I can't believe Merle would be so spineless. And Sasha! I thought you two were better friends than that. Shows how far loyalty will get you in this town."

"There are other apothecaries in Ambrey," Charl said. "I'll just have to hope that some of them will be interested. And I can mix up a few tinctures of my own to sell at the next market. There are a couple of recipes in my father's book." The thought of spending a day standing in the cold and fielding skeptical glances from villagers who bypassed her stall in favor of those they trusted more just made her want to go home and crawl into bed. Or maybe that was the exhaustion from her first outing since falling ill.

But as they crested the last rise and her house came into view, any thought of rest fled her mind. A large black coach sat in the yard, and figures in the blue uniform of the Magical Regulation Squad swarmed the grounds.

"Dirty fangs," she swore under her breath. She gripped Prax's hand on the reins. "Let me out here. I'll walk the rest of the way."

"What? No, I'll go with you—"

"You can't. The last thing either of us need is for you to attract their attention. Hopefully they won't learn that you took me to town today."

"Stop it, Charl," Prax snapped. "You're acting like them. If you act like you're hiding something, you'll convince them you are."

"But we *are* hiding something, Prax! What happens if they decide they need to search your place? Can you promise they won't find Forest?"

Prax paused, and she saw in his eyes the beginning of surrender.

"If you go home now," she continued, "they'll have no reason to suspect you. We're not far. I can walk without trouble."

"What about your jars?" he asked begrudgingly.

"I'll take one with me. Would you mind hanging onto the other for now?"

The ground was hard beneath her feet, and Charl knew that more frost was on the way. She didn't relish the idea of walking such a distance, but it was for the best. If Forest were discovered, it would be catastrophic for them both.

Still, Prax was reluctant to leave. "Are you sure you'll be okay? I don't like the idea of you facing those Regs alone."

Charl smiled a little and hefted the jar in her arms. "Why not? You said it yourself; I don't have anything to hide. You're the one harboring an illegal hatchling, remember?" And she turned her back before she could change her mind.

11

FACING THE REGS

By the time Charl reached the garden, her back strained under the awkwardness of carrying the jar down the lane. Two Regs were combing through the limp pumpkin vines and potato plants. Charl recognized one of them and stopped, resting the jar against the fence.

"Nice of you to come clean up for me, Therin. Why don't you grab a hoe and do the job properly?"

The man looked up and his black brows drew together in a scowl. He straightened and murmured to his companion, who followed suit.

"Don't get cheeky with me, Charlotte. They've got a warrant."

"Who's 'they?'"

He nodded toward the cottage as a man emerged. Indignation flared in her chest. They were in her home? Charl marched to the door trying to maintain as much dignity as possible, despite the weight of her burden making her gait uneven.

"Excuse me, sir," she demanded.

The man turned as she approached, and Charl faltered. In spite of hair cropped short in the way of soldiers, the face was distinctly feminine. She had olive skin and dark eyes that took in Charl and frowned.

"We're looking for Roland, dragon farmer of Ambrey," she said. "Are you his wife?"

"Sister," Charl corrected, looking over the woman's uniform with a twinge of awe. Her coat was more decorated than the other Regs, with insignias Charl had never seen before.

"Where is your brother?"

"I haven't a clue. He disappeared nine months ago. Therin knows that, though. He should have told you not to waste your time coming here to look for him."

The woman's eyes flickered to Therin who had approached as they talked, mud from Charl's garden clinging to his boots.

"You expect me to believe that he hasn't contacted you in any way in nine months? You have a valuable brood of dragons here. Who's been caring for them?"

"I have." Charl's cheeks warmed under the woman's look of skepticism. "And I don't know where my brother is. What's your interest in him, anyway?"

The woman ignored her, and looked at Therin. "How trustworthy is she?"

Charl bit back a retort and glared at Therin.

Therin's breath puffed out a long cloud. "I don't know how trustworthy any of these dragon farmers are, Captain. But she's never given me any trouble. Roland neither. Always pass inspection."

The captain's stoic expression didn't register the remark. She looked at the jar in Charl's arms. "What's that?"

"Egg drainings. I just came from the blacksmith."

"Get Slip," the captain commanded.

The door to the cottage opened again and another Reg stepped out. Charl's lips parted in alarm. He was holding her father's journal and Meirdan's book. The seam on the old spine strained dangerously under his rough hands.

"I found these," he said to the captain.

She took them, glancing briefly at Meirdan's history. Charl's father's journal earned more notice, and she thumbed through the pages more deliberately.

"Careful." Charl couldn't stop herself. "Please."

The captain looked up at her with a flash of humor in her eyes. "Why so protective?"

"It's my father's journal. There's over twenty years of experience in those pages. I need it to...it's important to me in my work."

"Your work? You're little more than a child," she said dismissively.

Charl's cheeks flamed. She wanted to point out that she hadn't been a child in years, not since her parents' deaths had put the hard labor of the farm on her and her brother with no one else to turn to for help. But looking at the captain's confident stance made her feel like she might as well have been in a short dress and pigtails by comparison.

"I do the best I can." Her voice sounded small in her own ears.

The captain ignored her, turning to the barn as the door opened. They'd been in the *barn?*

A man stepped out—this time she was sure it was a man—and Charl forgot her embarrassment. She'd never seen a trapper before, but she knew instinctively that's what he was. He wore a long sleeveless coat of black dragon skin that hung down to his knees and fastened across his chest with pieces of bone. Dragon teeth, she realized as he drew closer. His forearms were covered in sleeves of skin that stopped above the elbow so his thick biceps were visible. At his side hung a broadsword. A longbow was strapped across his back, a quiver visible above his shoulder.

As he approached, Charl recoiled, imagining her beloved dragons skinned for their hides. He saw her reaction and frowned. No, that wasn't right. A scar ran from the edge of his mouth, pulling his lips down into a frown. But his eyes were curious.

"This the farmer?"

"One of them," the captain said. "Check her jar."

He reached for it, and Charl didn't stop him. Any protest died in her throat as she stared at his large scar. It ran from his mouth down his jaw and disappeared under the high collar of his coat.

He opened the lid and held the jar up to his face. Closing his eyes, he breathed in deeply.

"Well?" the captain asked.

The trapper shook his head. "It's unfertilized. I'd wager it's the yarrowback."

Charl blinked. He could tell the egg was from Marin just by *smelling* it?

"Are you a seer?" she blurted.

"Don't be ridiculous," the captain snorted. "Slip's under the influence of faerie sand."

Charl looked at her to see if she was joking, but the captain's scowl seemed permanent on her face.

"But faerie sand is illegal."

"It's highly controlled," she replied dismissively. "Trappers have a special license to use it when they're on the hunt."

"Fortunately for us, a hunt can be quite lengthy," Slip said, and Charl thought she caught a twinkle in his eye. "You'd better get that separating soon. It's already going stale."

Charl seized the opportunity to back away from the man in dragon hide. She took the jar into the cottage and set it down on the table next to a mound of smooth brown dough Prax had left to rise. How much longer would the Regs stick around? Her back ached, and she needed rest. And with an illegal hatchling hiding only a few miles away, the Regs couldn't have come at a worse time.

12

CORRESPONDENCE

A movement at the door caught Charl's attention, and she looked up to find the captain standing in the doorway, silhouetted against the light.

"Why are you here?" Charl asked. "Therin says you have a warrant, but he didn't say what it's for. Am I under arrest?"

The captain answered with a question of her own. "Do you know a dragon breeder by the name of Larch? From the Pittock Range."

Charl shook her head.

"He was arrested two months ago on charges of illegal breeding. It seems he rents out his bulls for a steep price to farmers trying to increase their stock without a license. We're still hunting down his customers."

Charl reached for a pitcher of water and poured herself a tumbler. Bless Prax for thinking of everything. She didn't think she could draw water from the well after the exertions of the day.

"So this is a routine inspection?"

"This is hardly routine. What's your name, child?"

"Charlotte."

The captain stepped inside the cottage. She was taller than Charl, and Charl wondered briefly what her story was. How did a woman reach captain's rank? She'd never heard of such a thing, though in fairness she hadn't met any other captains all the way out here in Ambrey. Maybe in the capital city of Sorcester it wasn't so uncommon. She'd have to ask Prax.

"Let's sit for a moment, shall we?" The captain pulled out a wooden stool from under the table and gestured for Charl to sit.

Charl was more wary of the captain's sudden solicitous manner than she had been her earlier brusqueness. But she obeyed, relieved to get off her feet.

"Tell me about your family. Your parents have passed on, I assume?"

Charl nodded. "My father was Arthur of Ambrey. My mother was Petrica of Sorcester."

The captain arched one eyebrow. "This will go much easier if you answer honestly. I'm trying to give you the benefit of the doubt, but I have the power to arrest anyone who intentionally obstructs my investigation."

"I don't know what you mean. I answered

honestly. Those are my parents. My father's family have been dragon farmers for generations. My great-grandfather was the first to come to Ambrey, and we've been here ever since. My great-great-great-grandmother was Meirdan the Protector herself." She said it with pride, but the captain didn't seem impressed.

"Who were your mother's family?"

"Merchants from Sorcester. She met my father when he went there to meet with a breeder. He came home with both a blue-ridged razortail and a new bride." He'd always said meeting Charl's mother was the luckiest day of his life.

The captain was unmoved. "And Roland, he's your senior?"

"By a year. Our parents died two years back. Roland left nine months ago."

"Did you ever hear him talk about a man named Larch?"

"Not that I remember."

"Well, that's interesting. Because it seems that some time after your parents died, your brother entered into correspondence with Larch and brokered a deal for a bull."

Charl's back throbbed, and she felt lightheaded. "I don't believe it. Roland would never do anything so reckless. Not to mention that we never could have paid for it."

In answer, the captain pulled out a leather packet from her satchel and placed it on the table next to the bread dough.

"Here's one of his letters. Do you agree that's your brother's hand?"

Charl could scarcely read the script. Her eyes had trouble focusing and jumped over the page. But on the second page, she clearly recognized his signature.

"That looks like his signature, but it must be faked. I can't believe Roland would do this."

"We have dozens of letters like this, written over the course of nearly a year, detailing negotiations. Your brother claimed to have an everlight candle in his possession to barter with."

Charl's throat tightened. Had Roland sold her dowry to bring an illegal bull to mate with their dragons? It was so implausible she should have laughed it off.

If not for little Forest hiding in Prax's old dugout cellar.

She wanted to rush to the loft and check the hiding space under her mattress where the candle was hidden, but she didn't dare with the captain watching.

"These are just letters. They don't prove anything."

"That's why I'm here," the trapper said from the doorway. "If there's a dragon hiding in the area, I'll find him." He looked even more menacing darkening the doorway than he had out in the light.

Charl attempted confidence but worried it sounded more like panic. "You're wasting your time. Maybe Roland did write to this Larch, but I would know if he brought a male dragon here. That's not something you can hide."

"We'll see."

"Captain!" Therin's voice called from outside. "You'd better come see what we found."

Dread roiled in Charl's stomach as the captain followed the trapper out the door with short, clipped steps. She made herself stay seated, knowing she was more likely to betray herself if she didn't take time to compose a credible lie.

Through the open door she watched the trapper and captain huddle around Therin. Mist crept along the garden fence and past the empty goat pen, forming near their feet as the afternoon waned. She couldn't see what Therin held between them, but she didn't need to.

"Found it behind the house," Therin said. "What do you think?"

In the long silence that followed, Charl imagined the trapper holding the pail to his nose and smelling Forest's discarded shells. Why hadn't she buried them when she had the chance?

If he could distinguish a yarrowback from a razortail, she was doomed.

"It's too old. The membrane has dried. But it's a clean harvest. Definitely suggestive."

Charl breathed a hopeful sigh of relief.

The captain turned and stormed back through the door so fast that Charl shrank involuntarily. "You haven't been honest with us, Charlotte. Where's the hatchling that came from this egg?"

Charl gripped the table as she stood, feeling the smoothness of the wood worn by so many lives lived around its edge. "I don't know what you mean. Search the barn. There's no hatchling."

"Therin! Arrest her on charges of illegal dragon—"

"Hold on, Wynne." The trapper laid a hand on the captain's shoulder. "We don't have proof there was a hatchling. I'll take the shells with me. I have methods that can extract enough of the membrane to be definitive."

The captain glared at him, then turned her scowl to Charl. "Fine. But I warn you, Charlotte, if I find that you've been lying to us, I'll charge you with the lot. Breeding, smuggling, interfering with a Regulation investigation. You'll never see the light of day again."

She marched out of the cottage, and Charl sank back onto the stool, her legs unsteady. Whatever courage she'd managed to muster had been drained out of her. All that was left was certain dread.

13
TRAPPER

Charl crumpled, her head in her hands, and closed her eyes against the despair that squeezed her throat. The creak of a floorboard made her realize she wasn't alone. Her eyes flew open, and she looked up to find the trapper was still there, watching her.

"If I'm not mistaken," he began, his voice deep and calm, "you've suffered an injury recently. Am I right?"

"The faerie sand?" Charl guessed.

"No." His mouth twitched like he wanted to smile. "In my profession I spend a lot of time tending to dragon injuries. I may be able to help."

Charl peered at him, uncertain what to think. "Why would you help me? Isn't that a conflict of interest?"

Now he did smile, but the scar turned it into a lopsided smirk. He straddled the nearest stool where

Wynne had sat. Charl struggled to look away from the dragon teeth across his chest.

"Call me Slip," he said. "I'm not a Reg, and I don't care whether you go to prison. That's up to Wynne and makes no difference to me. My job is to find all of Larch's dragons. I don't see why helping you would conflict with that. Besides, there are few enough of us as it is."

"There's no 'us.' Trappers and farmers aren't the same. A trapper is just a glorified slayer." Slayers were technically illegal, the term used to describe rogue poachers who were usually poorly trained and subverted the restrictions licensed trappers were required to follow. To Charl, the difference was negligible. The end result was the same: dead dragons.

Slip didn't seem offended. Instead, he looked amused. "How do you think farmers domesticated dragons in the first place without trappers? I saw the ropes and spears in your barn. Where do you think farmers learned those techniques?"

Charl opened her mouth to protest, then closed it again. There was no point in arguing. A man like Slip wouldn't understand. Besides, she was long overdue for a bandage change.

As if he read her mind, Slip asked, "Do you have any dalg root?"

"No dalg. I've been making hendel tea."

"Hendel without dalg? No wonder you're moving so stiff. Tell me what happened." He looked her over with a critical eye, and Charl fought the urge to move away.

"It's my back. Stella grazed me with her talon, and it got infected with oil."

Slip tsked sympathetically. "Does she normally produce an excess of oil when laying?"

"I guess. I don't know." Charl wondered if she'd already said too much. Better not let on that Stella was broody.

"Let me take a look."

Just talking about it made the pain flare insistently, but Charl couldn't bring herself to let him touch her.

"Well...I don't know you and..." She trailed off, her face burning.

"Ah, of course." Slip went to the door and called out, "Wynne! I need a hand."

Captain Wynne came in, glowering at them both. Charl wasn't sure this was an improvement, but at least Wynne wasn't dressed in dead dragon trophies.

"What is it?" Wynne asked tightly.

"Help Charlotte with her shirt so I can dress her wound."

"What wound?"

In answer, Charl turned her back to Slip and untied the lacing of her shirt to loosen the neckline. She eased her arms out of the sleeves carefully and by the time she'd finished with the first one, Wynne had stepped forward, helping with the second. Charl hugged her shirt against her chest, wondering how she came to be half-dressed in the presence of two enemies.

Wynne's hands were cold and brisk as she

unwrapped the bandages from around Charl's shoulder and torso. When she pulled the last layer away, the fabric caught in the stitches. Charl bit back a moan of pain.

Slip whistled. "Who stitched it for you?"

"My neighbor," Charl said through clenched teeth, panting against the pain.

Wynne snorted. "Your neighbor is no surgeon."

"The job's done well enough," Slip said gamely, but it sounded forced.

Charl hugged her middle, the chilly air prickling her exposed skin and raising gooseflesh. When something cold and wet touched her back, she hissed.

"Hold still," Slip said soothingly. "This is a light dalg salve, my own recipe. It'll do wonders."

Charl closed her eyes, tense with the effort of keeping still. His touch was gentle but efficient, and soon he leaned back and sighed with satisfaction.

"Ready for you, Wynne."

Wynne replaced the bandages with clean ones Prax had washed and left by Charl's bed. She worked quickly, if not with any tenderness. Charl could almost feel the hostility oozing from her.

As soon as she was finished, Wynne said sourly, "If you're finished playing nursemaid, Slip, we've got work to do." She strode out of the house, leaving the door open for Slip to follow.

But Slip lingered, grating something into a bowl.

"Add this to your hendel tea. It'll help with the stiffness."

"Thank you," Charl answered, tying her shirt

closed again. But she felt off balance, wondering what his motivation was.

She tried not to stare at Slip's thick scar, repulsed by how it distorted his smile. How long had it taken Prax to get used to the scar that had nearly cost Charl her eye?

"Your dragons. Do they roost in the barn?"

Slip stood in the open doorway. Beyond him, dusk was beginning to creep into the forest at the edge of the garden. Charl was so tired. Now that the salve was beginning to lessen some of the pain, all she wanted to do was rest.

"I'll help if you'd like," Slip offered, and took off across the yard before she could object.

Charl roused herself and followed, struggling to keep up. They passed Wynne crouched over the bucket of shell fragments. She was taking notes in a ledger of some kind and shot Slip a dark look as they passed.

Charl stopped at the barn door, one hand on the latch. She could smell the dragon hide from Slip's coat. "You can't go in there dressed like that. They'll tear you apart."

"I can handle myself, farmer."

"That may be, but they're my dragons, and I don't want them getting worked into a frenzy."

"How sentimental of you."

"It's practical, not sentimental," Charl snapped. "If they get distressed, I pay the price."

"Is that what happened to your back?" Slip's eyes were gray and keen, and she found herself struggling to meet them. If not for the scar, he might have been handsome.

Charl ignored the question. "Are you always this annoying? Don't say I didn't warn you," she said as she pushed the door open.

Fading daylight illuminated the barn from the small clerestory windows near the ceiling. Scratching at the cave door announced that the dragons were ready to settle in for the night.

"Help me with the corn," Charl said, opening the cellar door to reveal the sacks of grain.

"You don't feed them corn all winter, do you?"

"Only when Regs invade my property so I'm not able to tend my traps."

The barrel was almost empty now, so Slip heaved a sack of corn to the trough and Charl cut the bindings.

"Has anyone told you how unusual your eyes are?" Slip asked as he joined Charl at the entrance to the cave.

She ignored him, sliding the bar to unlatch the doors. Slip pulled while she pushed, and she was grateful for his strength, even if his comments were getting tiresome.

The dragons knew immediately that something was amiss. Stella stood in the entrance to the cave and arched her wings threateningly. She thrust her snout toward Slip, hissing as she took in his scent. Marin and Iris followed suit behind her.

Slip's hand went to his sword.

"Don't!" Charl warned. "Just back away. Whatever you do, don't draw your sword. Come on, Stella. Get some food." She tried to keep her tone light, but her stomach was tight. For all her cavalier words, she didn't want to see Slip get mauled to death.

Stella stomped forward, her muscles taut.

Slip seemed not to notice her bared teeth and instead focused on her eyes with an intensity that made Charl want to cower. Stella snarled and crouched low. But before Charl could warn Slip to watch her whipping tail, he'd already leapt out of the way and her tail harmlessly coiled back on itself. Slip was agile and light-footed, inhumanly so.

The faerie sand, Charl realized.

He anticipated Stella's movements before Charl did, and Charl had known Stella her whole life. Stella reared back in frustration when a quick snap of her jaws was met with open air. And then, apparently deciding the trapper wasn't worth the trouble, she swung around and went to the pile of feed across the room.

Charl breathed a sigh of relief when Marin and Iris did little more than huff in annoyance at the visitor before turning to their food.

You see? Slip's expression seemed to say. He swatted Marin's tail as she passed.

"Stop bullying my dragons," Charl said in annoyance.

"They're dragons, Charlotte. Man's worst enemy. Or have you forgotten?"

"These dragons aren't anyone's enemies. They've

supported my family for generations. They deserve respect."

"You *are* sentimental," he observed. "Careful. That kind of talk could cause you even more trouble than you're already in."

"Why? Because I care about the well-being of my brood? Look around. I'm a farmer, Slip." She gathered up the feed sack and scooped out the last of the corn that had settled into a corner of the bag. "Make yourself useful and close the door."

Iris's black tongue shot out between her teeth and licked up the feed before it left Charl's hand. Rough and wet, her tongue scraped Charl's chest and face as well.

"Ugh. Thanks, Iris." Charl wiped her face and rubbed her hands on her legs. Now she smelled like corn *and* dragon spit.

She hoped Slip hadn't seen. But when she turned to him, her embarrassment gave way to something else. He was standing with one foot inside the cave, peering intently into the darkness. Charl felt a flare of alarm.

"Slip, let's go."

He looked at her, but his eyes seemed focused somewhere else. His silence was disconcerting.

"Are you going to close the door?"

He shook himself and grabbed the heavy door, pulling it closed. Charl didn't dare ask what had captured his attention.

Wynne was waiting for them outside, her eyes hooded in the advancing dark.

"Are you quite finished, Trapper?"

"I am now," Slip said.

Charl watched them climb into the coach and waited for relief to come. But something about Slip's tone—and the way he'd stared into the cave—made her fear that he was far from finished.

14
NIGHT VISITOR

Charl had little appetite, but she boiled up a handful of turnips, knowing that some of her weakness was from an empty stomach. She'd been a fool not to bury Forest's eggshells right away. But how could she have guessed that Roland was involved in something that would bring Regs to her doorstep?

At least they didn't know about Prax. Even if they learned the truth about the hatchling, there was no reason for suspicion to fall on him. She'd have to keep it that way.

Charl sat before the fireplace and ate her turnips slowly. If the Regs returned, she needed a convincing story that would keep her out of trouble. But she'd never been a very good liar.

Her eyes were heavy and she wasn't sure what time it was, but the fire was little more than embers now. The early night sounds of frogs had diminished long before. Wind sighed down the chimney and rattled the door with occasional gusts. A storm was brewing.

Charl thought of the previous winter when they were trapped for days while a blizzard howled outside. Roland had invented a guessing game for them to play that got increasingly complicated as it went along. Laughing with him had staved off boredom, but now the memory was tinged with pain. He'd disappeared only three days later.

She tried to imagine how Roland might have brought a bull to the farm right under her nose without her suspecting a thing. With a chill, she imagined Roland trying to lead a bull into the cave, vulnerable and unprotected. What if the dragon had spooked? What if it had attacked?

No, not attacked.

The dragon had been interested in the human, but not as a meal.

He'd reminded him of *her*.

Into her mind came the image of the woman she'd dreamed of, the one with the eyes flecked with gold. She stood at the edge of a ring of firelight, looking out into the night. A spear was in her hand and a helmet on her head as if she were prepared for battle.

Something thumped against the door, and Charl blinked, clearing her head. Another thump. Was it the wind, or had the Regs returned? She shuffled to the door and paused. There was a faint tap that was definitely not the wind.

"Charl? Are you there?"

Charl slid the bolt and cracked open the door. Prax stood on her stoop, face shadowed by a hooded cloak.

"Prax, you shouldn't be here."

"Can I come in?"

Charl hesitated as dry leaves gusted through the open door. She shouldn't let him in, especially if the Regs returned. But if she got arrested in the morning, would this be the last time they had together? Cursing herself for her own weakness, she moved aside and opened the door.

He smelled of the oncoming storm as he ducked inside.

"It's not safe for you here," she chided. "You shouldn't have come."

"Where's your light?" he replied, ignoring her.

She heard the scrape of a tinder box and then a candle sparked to light. It cast a pale circle of light on the table and threw shadows on the contours of Prax's face. He made a show of looking her over.

"I don't see any shackles, so your visit with the Regs must have gone well."

"Hardly."

In spite of her earlier commitment to not involve him further, she found herself spilling all the details of the Regs' search. They sat at the hearth and while Prax coaxed the embers back to life, Charl told him of Roland's letters, the eggshells, and the trapper.

Prax frowned at this. "They think you're hiding a dragon?"

"Well, I mean, there is Forest..."

Prax rubbed a hand over his face. "Of course. Charl, what can I do to help?"

"Nothing. We just have to hope that whatever tests Slip is doing, the shells are old enough to not tell him anything."

"Slip?" Prax looked at her sharply.

"The trapper. Have you heard of him?"

Prax grunted. "Yeah, I know who he is. They must really be worried if they called him in."

Charl shivered. "If there's a bull hidden in the cave, I want him found. But they'll think I was part of it. Nothing I could say would convince them otherwise."

Prax considered this, leaning forward to rest his elbows on his knees. After a moment, he asked softly, "Are you angry at Roland?"

Charl hesitated, then shook her head. "I was at first. But now I'm just worried. Did he run away because he knew he was going to be discovered? Why not tell me so I could help? Or was he trying to protect me? I can't help but worry that something terrible happened to him. If he's living fat and rich on the islands of Cerise, then I'll be angry. But also relieved, you know?"

Prax nodded. In the silence that followed, Charl noticed for the first time the day's stubble lining his jaw. Her hand was close to his. The thought made her heart skip a beat.

Could she be brave enough to reach out and take it? If she were arrested in the morning, would it be better or worse if her last words to him were confessing how she felt? Would she regret not telling him that their days together had been her happiest since her parents were alive?

Prax shifted, turning to face her. As if reading her thoughts, he reached for her hands and held them in his own. His eyes were shadowed as the firelight played across his features, but his voice was earnest.

"Charl, there's something I need to tell you. This might not be the best time, but I keep putting it off, thinking I'll have another chance. But with everything going on, I'm not so sure."

Charl's breath stilled. Her heart raced like a wind sprite in a summer storm. Hope warmed her, but it was tinged with grief. Why now? Why would he choose *this* moment when she stood on the edge of a possible life prison sentence?

His thumb rubbed against an old scar on the back of her hand, and he looked at it as if nervous to meet her eyes. "I don't know how to say this...but you are more special than you know. I should have told you months ago, but I didn't want to do anything to ruin our friendship. And I didn't know if you would want to hear what I have to say."

Charl's lips parted in disbelief. Could he really feel the same way she did?

He finally raised his eyes to hers, and in them she saw pain. "I just want you to know that no matter what happens—"

A loud thump at the door startled them both.

"Open this door in the name of the king!"

It was Captain Wynne.

Charl's heart leaped in panic. No, not now. Couldn't she let her have this one moment? She looked at Prax and made her decision. Quickly, she leaned forward and pressed her lips to his. He stiffened in shock, but then relaxed into the kiss and moved his hands to cup her jaw.

The pounding on the door returned, but Charl gave herself to this moment with Prax, ignoring everything except the smell of his skin and the feel of his lips against hers.

It was over too soon. Charl pulled away, feeling heady and disoriented. Prax's eyes were bright.

"Charl, I—"

"Hide," she commanded him. "Up in the loft. If you lay in the space on the far edge of the mattress, they might not see you."

"I'm not going anywhere," he insisted, standing by her side.

"Charlotte Dragon farmer, if you don't open this door, we can't be held responsible for damages!"

"Please," she begged, moving to the door. "You don't deserve to be caught up in this."

"I'm sorry, but I can't."

The look in his eyes filled her with a surge of something powerful that gave her strength to open the door and face Captain Wynne.

15
CHIVALRY

Charl opened the door, but Wynne wasn't there. She'd stepped back to make room for a Reg with a large axe who was winding up to strike the door.

"Whoa!" Charl cried. "I'm here, all right?"

"Stand down," Wynne said curtly to the soldier. She pushed her way into the room and stopped when she saw Prax. "Who are you?" she demanded.

"This is my neighbor," Charl said.

Wynne looked him up and down appraisingly. "A little late for a friendly chat. What's your name?"

Prax seemed uncertain how to respond to Wynne's aggressive tone. Charl rushed to his side and pulled on his sleeve, trying to usher him to the door.

"His name is Praxton. He came to check on me, but he was just leaving."

"Praxton? Is this the same neighbor who stitched up your back?"

"Yes. He's very thoughtful. But whatever you need doesn't concern him—"

"You don't know that. Where do you live, Praxton?"

"Captain!" Charl snapped. "If you're going to arrest me, get on with it. But leave Prax out of it. He's just a kind man helping someone in need. Please, let him go."

"What do you think, Slip?" Wynne said, looking over Charl's shoulder at the door.

Slip stood there, looking formidable in a long cloak made of dragon skin. Was his whole wardrobe made of the creatures' hides? Disgusting.

Slip looked at Prax, and a distorted smile spread across his face.

"Well. Aren't you full of surprises, farmer? Praxton, is it?"

Something in his tone sounded taunting, and Charl hated him for it.

"Please, Slip. He has nothing to do with any of this."

"I wouldn't count on that." Slip looked at her, and his eyes widened. He looked back and forth between them and laughed cruelly. "No. You can't be serious."

The color rushed back into Prax's cheeks, and he finally found his voice. "I won't let you take Charl. You have no right to accuse her for her brother's crimes."

"Is that right? How lucky Charl is to have such a solicitous neighbor."

Wynne looked back and forth between Slip and Prax. "What's going on here?"

"Do you want to tell her, Praxton?" Slip jeered. "Or shall I?"

Charl blushed. Prax wouldn't meet her eyes. Whatever Slip thought their relationship was, he was wrong. And he was destroying any hope she had of it becoming more by making a mockery of them both.

"I think Charlotte hasn't been truthful about the nature of her relationship with her neighbor. Or maybe he's the one who hasn't been truthful with her?"

"So? What does this have to do with dragons?" Wynne barked.

Slip shrugged. "Probably nothing."

"Then let's focus on the matter at hand." Wynne turned to Charl with a glimmer of triumph in her eye. "Charlotte, Dragon farmer of Ambrey, we have reason to believe that you have recently hatched a fertilized dragon egg in violation of Section XVII of the Magical Regulation Code. Accordingly, I have the authority to arrest you and bring you to Sorcester where you will await trial for illegally breeding a Class A restricted creature."

The words made Charl's head spin. She forced herself to stare into Wynne's dark eyes instead of looking at Prax. She didn't dare betray more than she already had.

"However," Wynne continued, and Charl's heart skipped a beat. *However?* "The specific latitude I've been given for this mission allows me to exercise clemency under certain conditions." Her commanding tone softened to something a little more human. "I'm less worried about throwing you in jail than I am tracking down Larch's hidden dragons and any offspring they may have produced."

Charl's mouth went dry. "I already told you I don't know anything about Larch or his dragons. If Roland was working with him, he kept it to himself."

"And the hatchling? Where is it?"

Charl could feel Prax's eyes on her, and only with great effort did she avoid glancing his way. "I found the eggshells in the cave one morning when I opened the door. I never saw any hatchling, and I don't know where it is. I took the shells and angered the mother in the process, which earned me a slash across the back." She'd thought of the excuse earlier that evening and hoped it didn't sound too practiced.

"And you didn't think to report it?" Wynne said skeptically.

"Report what? How was I supposed to know the egg was fertilized? Not to mention that this is the first I've been able to leave the house in almost a week."

Wynne looked to Slip for corroboration.

He nodded. "It fits."

"So either way, it sounds like we're going into the cave," Wynne said with a sigh.

"Either way?" Charl asked.

Wynne smiled, but it held no warmth. "We've still got to find out if there's a dragon hidden in there. And you're going to help us."

"Me?" Now Charl did risk a look at Prax and saw the same shock on his face.

"This is your cave. Who better to guide us through it?"

"But I've never been in the cave. It's for the dragons; we don't go inside. I couldn't lead you any better than you could lead yourselves!" And then Charl realized. It wasn't about her. It was about providing another warm body who could potentially distract the bull. She wasn't an asset. She was bait.

"That's my offer, farmer. You prove your innocence and earn your freedom by helping us, or you submit to arrest."

Charl couldn't believe the woman could issue the threat so calmly. Did faerie blood run in her veins that she could be so disinterested in the welfare of another human being?

Slip frowned and opened his mouth as if he wanted to say something, but then closed it again and remained silent.

"You don't have to do this, Charl," Prax said, but there was a tension in his voice that sounded like fear. "There's got to be another way."

"There is no other way," Wynne said. "Ask Slip. This is as generous as I get. Take it or leave it."

"It's true," Slip agreed. "I know what you're thinking, Charl. You're thinking that Wynne intends to feed you to the bull. I can't say that won't be the outcome—it could be how it ends for all of us—but I think you're a lot more valuable than that. You know your dragons and smell like them. He'll recognize their scent and may be more cooperative. And it's always nice to have someone who knows how to read dragon moods. You're more useful to me alive than dead. I, for one, won't actively promote your death."

Charl gaped. *That* was supposed to sound comforting?

Prax shook his head. "Don't do this, Charl. A trial would be better than this."

"It might be helpful if she had influential friends, but she's a poor farmer from Ambrey," Slip said, his tone mocking again. "Who would come to her aid?"

Prax pressed his lips together but his eyes stormed with anger.

Charl looked at Wynne and Slip. If she were arrested, she was certain Prax would be under suspicion, especially now that Slip thought they were more...involved than they were. If they found Forest, then her fate would be sealed. And Prax's too.

But if she cooperated and survived the ordeal, there was a chance for them both.

"I'll do it," she said.

Prax's shoulders sank. "Charl." It was almost a whisper.

"That's settled then," Wynne said brusquely. "Gather your things. We leave as soon as you're ready."

Charl moved to let her pass and stepped closer to Prax. "Will you watch over things here for me while I'm gone?"

Prax sighed and shook his head. "I'm sorry, I can't do that. Captain!" he called.

Wynne stopped in the open doorway.

"I'm coming too."

"What?" Charl cried. "Prax, don't be a soft-scale. You have to stay here where it's safe. You have to take care of things. Please."

By *things* she meant Forest, and by *take care of* she meant *your life depends on not letting anyone find out, so don't be an idiot and get all chivalrous on me.*

Prax ignored her. He held Wynne's gaze in challenge. "If Charl goes, I go."

Slip smiled. "So protective."

A muscle twitched along Wynne's jawline. "Do you know how to wield a sword or spear?"

"I'm fair enough with a sword," Prax said. "If you have one to spare."

"More than fair, I'd wager," Slip taunted, picking up Charl's pot with the leftover turnips. He sniffed at the leavings and grimaced.

Wynne shrugged. "Suit yourself. It'll be standard Reg issue, nothing custom." She strode out into the night, and the breeze in her wake smelled of fresh rain. The storm was close.

Charl stared at Prax. "When have you ever wielded a sword?" she whispered.

"I wasn't always a farmer," Prax murmured. "Do you have a knapsack? I'll carry supplies for the both of us so you don't have to strain your back."

As if in reply, Charl's back flared with pain. Maybe a little chivalry was a good idea after all.

16

DRAGON HUNT

While Prax gathered supplies into Roland's old knapsack, Charl climbed the ladder to the loft. Rain had started, whispering on the thatched roof overhead.

Her mattress smelled old and stale since she'd skipped the autumn stuffing. She'd been sleeping in Roland's bed since the summer, and there didn't seem a point in wasting the extra straw. Her tender back protested as she lifted the corner that obscured her hiding place in the floor. She found the loose nail and pried it up with her fingernails, then reached into the dark for the wooden box, relieved that it was still there.

Whatever promises Roland had made, he hadn't sold her everlight.

When she came back down the stairs, Prax looked at her with interest.

"What's that?"

In answer, she reached for the tin lantern that sat

on the windowsill. The old candle had diminished to no more than a stub. She pried it out and opened the box.

The everlight lay against a backdrop of black velvet, like the pale arm of one of the northern people whose skin was rumored to be as light as linen. Its wick was untarnished, and Charl felt as if she were desecrating something holy when she took it out of the box and placed it in the lantern.

"Is that what I think it is?" Prax asked.

Slip was stirring something in a pot and looked up.

"Papa said to save it for a special occasion, but I think he meant a *happier* special occasion," Charl said with a sad smile.

"So you *do* have an everlight after all? Wynne will be interested to hear that." Slip commented as he added the bits of dalg he'd shaved during his earlier visit.

"Are you sure about this?" Prax asked. "You could sell it and live for years—"

"I can't sell it in Ambrey. No one could give me what it's worth. I'd have to take it to Sorcester, and I can't do that if I'm in prison."

"But Charl—"

"We need all the help we can get. If we get trapped in that cave without light, we'll never make it out alive."

"Not a problem with faerie sand," Slip said. "I never lose my way."

"Good for you," Charl retorted. "But that's no

guarantee for us, is it?" She grabbed the tinder box decisively.

When the wick flared to life, it seemed to do so angrily, as if chiding Charl for letting down her family and wasting their most precious possession. The flame danced at first, then settled into a steady glow of pale yellow. Charl watched it for a moment to satisfy herself that it wouldn't consume the wax. The candle remained unchanged.

Charl closed the lantern briskly, hoping the others wouldn't see how much it pained her. *Roland tried to sell it,* she reminded herself. *It's his fault you're using it now.* But she couldn't help feeling like she was betraying her parents' hopes in some way.

Slip poured his concoction into a skin and the last traces into a tumbler. He gave the skin to Prax and the tumbler to Charl.

"Drink this down now, and then more before the pain gets too bad. If you can keep the pain under control, it doesn't take much."

Charl sniffed the tumbler warily.

Prax's expression darkened. He didn't trust Slip. Charl understood why he wouldn't like him—she didn't either and could barely stand the smell of dead dragon hide—but she also knew liking someone wasn't necessary to trust them. Slip was the only one outside of her family she'd ever met who had experience with dragons. Even though his profession went against everything she valued, she still felt a certain connection with him just because he understood her life in a way no one else did.

He *knew.*

She sipped the tea. She could still taste the hendel, but the overall flavor was more nutty than before.

Wynne returned with a sword for Prax, and they stepped outside where he could better test its heft and reach.

"How long has it been?" Wynne asked Prax as the door closed behind them.

Charl didn't hear the answer, but she marveled that Wynne sounded legitimately interested instead of simply annoyed. Like the villagers in Ambrey, Wynne had warmed to Prax in a way she hadn't to Charl. Maybe it should have bothered her, but Charl was used to feeling like a wood imp at every gathering, unwelcome and unwanted.

"Finished?" Slip asked, checking his own gear and tightening laces.

Well, maybe not *every* gathering. It didn't exactly make her feel better that Slip seemed so ready to accept her.

"How do you feel?" he asked.

The pain had eased, but the familiar clouding of her mind didn't come.

"Better," she admitted.

He nodded. "All right, Charl—do you mind if I call you Charl?"

"Fine."

"Very well, then. Ready for your first dragon hunt?"

Charl's stomach soured, and she regretted

drinking the tea so quickly. A descendant of Meirdan the Protector hunting dragons? She was a disgrace.

She grimaced and reached for Roland's leather coat and boots.

Outside, Prax and Wynne were sparring lightly. Charl frowned. Prax looked fair enough, not that she knew what to look for. She wondered what he had done before turning to farming. She'd never asked, assuming he'd been born to it the way she was.

Guided by the everlight, Charl crossed the yard, ducking her head against the rain. She stopped at the door of the barn, waiting for the others to catch up.

"He's good," Wynne told Slip approvingly.

Slip caught Charl's eye and winked.

She blushed and turned to the door. "Ready?"

The lantern cast a wide circle of light on the dirt floor as she stepped into the barn, but the rafters were deep in shadow. Charl listened closely over the sounds of the rain before letting the others in. She didn't want to be surprised by a grumpy hen stalking the intruders for sport. Deep breathing drifted down from above their heads. The dragons were asleep.

She moved aside to let the others pass. Prax came last, whispering a quiet, "I'll get the next one."

While he led the way to the cave door, she grabbed a wooden spear. It wouldn't be much use against dragon hide, but it was all she had.

Looking at her armed companions, she felt woefully unprepared.

The cave door groaned as Prax pulled it open, but he didn't have to pull it far to let the humans pass.

Still, Charl held her breath until it was closed safely behind them. Once on the other side, she listened for the sound of dragons but heard nothing over the pounding of blood in her ears.

"We should have brought food with us," she realized, turning to face the cavern. Her whisper slipped away from her into the empty space, and she wished she could take it back. The roof soared above them, and the light from the candle didn't penetrate the darkness overhead.

"We did bring food," Wynne muttered.

"No. I mean, for the dragons. If we come back and they're hungry, it would have helped to distract them."

"Oh. Right," Prax said.

"I guess it all depends on if we do come back," Slip said cheerily.

Prax reached for her hand and squeezed. She squeezed back gratefully.

"So, where should we start?"

17
INTO THE DARK

Hours passed interminably in the cave. Charl was grateful for the everlight, but it didn't chase away the feeling of rock pressing overhead or the yawning black which lurked around every corner. The cavern felt so open and exposed that she was glad when Slip led them down a corridor branching off the main entrance. More tunnels branched off this one, leading to alcoves and dead ends, and it wasn't long before Charl started to doubt her sense of direction. Prax looked uneasy the further they explored, and even Captain Wynne grew quieter the more time passed. It would be easy to get lost in the caves and never find their way back.

Slip was the only one who seemed unaffected by the dark. Charl knew he was still using the faerie sand —she'd seen him slip some under his tongue—and she wondered if that helped keep away the gloom of the cave.

"Too many dragons," he muttered when the ceiling lowered until they were crawling.

"What's that?" Wynne asked.

"It's hard to smell anything but the females."

"Did we go the wrong way, then?" Charl asked hopefully. Wynne's boots were in her face and the rock was hard beneath her knees.

Slip didn't answer. Wynne stopped crawling, and Charl peered around her. Slip was flat on his stomach, one hand held out in warning.

Charl looked back at Prax. He shook his head.

"If we can't get through here, the dragons couldn't either, could they?"

His voice was only a whisper, but Slip shushed him.

Charl sat back on her heels to give her knees a rest, and wondered what Slip was listening for.

Prax sidled closer. "How are you feeling? Do you need to rest?"

Charl shook her head. The dalg root was helping, but more than anything she didn't want Prax to worry.

A skittering sound drew her attention. Slip was shifting his body in the tight space. "We're going to need to find another way around." His dark tone suggested he didn't like it. "There's something on the other side."

"The dragons couldn't have come this way, though," Charl said, voicing Prax's argument.

"They don't have to. But we don't have wings so we're stuck finding a different route."

It was easier to back up than to turn around in the tight space, but Charl felt more than a little ridiculous shuffling backward on her knees. When the buckle on Wynne's belt started tinkling in rhythm, Charl snorted a laugh.

Wynne's glare could have frozen a kettle in full steam.

Charl tried to suppress another giggle, but it burst out of her. "I'm sorry! I just expected a dragon hunt would feel more dignified."

Prax hid a smile.

"Get moving, farmer," Wynne snapped, "or you'll get my boot in your teeth."

"Hey, there's no call for that," Prax objected. "A little humor never hurt anyone."

"It did when they announced their presence long before they reached the dragon they were hunting," Slip said.

This quelled Charl's mirth. She shouldn't be here. She would give them away and get them all killed. She finished crawling out of the tunnel in silence.

When they could stand again, Charl began dusting her knees off then stopped when she noticed the others didn't seem bothered by the fine gray dirt coating their clothes.

"Now what?"

"We find another way," Slip said simply and strode back the way they had come.

Wynne followed, her spine rigid with resentment,

but Charl hung back with Prax, slowing her pace so they had a semblance of privacy.

"Where did you learn to use a sword? What did you do before you were a farmer?"

Prax smiled without amusement. "My father required me to train. All of my siblings too. Some of them really took to it. Two of my brothers joined the Royal Guard, and my sister served for a while as private guard to the Ambassador to the Faeries."

"You're joking!"

"No. My father was very exacting." He said it bitterly, in a way that made Charl swallow the questions that had risen in her throat.

As they walked, she watched him out of the corner of her eye, looking for a hint of a fighter. But the only soldiers she knew were the local Regs, whose bellies sagged over their sword belts. The only time she saw them use their steel was for beating the long grass in the summer to scare up snakes.

Prax had the lean build of a farmer—strong, yes, but also living just a few meals shy of starving. Still, Wynne had pronounced him good enough at sparring, and Charl suspected she wouldn't give such praise if she didn't mean it.

A sense of awe washed over Charl. When Prax noticed her watching him, she blushed.

"What's that look for?" he asked.

"I'm wondering what your family thought when you decided to come to Ambrey and be a farmer. Is that why you never speak of them?" It was partly true. Somewhere thoughts of his family had mixed in there.

"They supported my decision, but I won't deny the distance has been good for us both." He wouldn't meet her eye as he said it, and she wondered what else he wasn't saying.

She wanted to ask more, but they rounded a corner and she realized they'd fallen too far behind. Slip and Wynne were nowhere in sight.

Charl stopped. They stood in a large open hall, half blocked by a rockfall, with deep shadows that hinted at tunnels and hidden chambers gouged into the walls high above their heads. Water ran in rivulets down the walls, leaving white and yellow deposits that shone in the lantern light.

"I don't remember this place," Prax said.

"Do you feel that?" Charl asked as a breeze brushed her face. "The air is moving. Somewhere, there's an outlet."

"And the smell? That's not the smell of your dragons." Prax's eyes were alight.

Charl closed her eyes and tried to clear her mind. For a moment she wished for some of Slip's faerie sand. The smell was both familiar and foreign, like something she should have known but had forgotten.

The everlight flickered behind her eyelids, and she tried to see past it into the dark. It was dense and cloying, and something moved out of sight. Something sinuous.

Daughter of Meirdan.

Charl gasped. Her eyes snapped open.

"What is it?" Prax asked, looking at her in alarm.

Charl shook her head, trying to shake the feeling of the voice in her mind. "We should leave." She started making her way around the rockfall, but Prax grabbed her arm.

"Where are you going? We have no way of knowing which direction they went."

Charl's heart raced. They couldn't be lost. They couldn't be...

"This way."

"How do you know?"

"I just do." Did she? Was that certainty that guided her steps or desperation? She couldn't tell Prax what she had seen. What she had heard.

She didn't know what she was looking for until she found it, a large boulder that looked as though it had triggered the fall, like a cork popped from a bottle. She walked around the boulder, its rough surface scraping her hands and leaving behind a fine dust. Where the boulder rested against the wall, a crack yielded a darker shadow that hinted of greater depths beyond.

"There's another tunnel back here."

"Of course there is." Prax sighed. "There will always be another tunnel, Charl. We need a plan. Wynne and Slip couldn't have come this way, they would have had to move those rocks first. We need to find them."

Charl knew he was right. Wynne she could do without, but she knew their best chances of survival were if they stayed with Slip.

"All right. Can we rest first? I'm so tired I can barely think straight."

Prax frowned at the pile of broken rock. Then he scanned the walls, and his expression cleared. "That might work."

A short distance away, a bulge in the cave wall formed a shelf above their heads, with boulders acting as makeshift stools to reach it.

"Give me the lantern," Prax said as he climbed the boulders. Once he pulled himself to the ledge, Charl passed him the lantern and he disappeared from view, taking the light with him.

Charl shivered in the darkness, trying not to imagine a creature watching her, waiting for a chance to spring. Was that its breath she felt on her neck?

"Prax?"

What was taking him so long?

At last, the light appeared.

"I'm here. Come on up. It's safe."

She handed him her spear and carefully clambered up the rough boulders. The dalg root really was helping, but her back still ached something fierce. When she reached the shelf, Prax gripped her arms and pulled her up. She was panting by the time she got to her feet, reminded of how much weaker she was from days of sickness.

A little way back, the ledge opened up into a small alcove, about the size of her loft in the cottage. The ground underfoot was sandy, and the roof was closed off overhead without being suffocating.

Sheltering. Nothing could sneak up on them from behind.

She sighed with relief.

They had a quiet meal of dried cakes and goat cheese, then Prax stretched out on the sandy floor, his eyelids drooping. Charl lay on the other side of the small chamber with the everlight between them. Neither one of them suggested covering it with the shield. Charl only wished it offered warmth against the persistent chill of the cave as she pulled her coat around her.

She listened to Prax's breathing slow and deepen, distracted by his nearness. She'd never slept in the same room with a man who wasn't her brother. And Prax didn't feel anything like a brother.

She thought of the hasty kiss they'd shared and the scrape of his whiskers against her lips. He'd enjoyed it too, right? She'd been impetuous, and it had been too short, but she didn't think it had been unwelcome.

She hoped.

Charl closed her eyes but couldn't rest. Somewhere water dripped in the stillness. Even in the darkness of her mind she felt that something was watching her from the shadows.

It *knew* her.

Again she saw the woman with eyes so like her own standing at the edge of a ring of firelight, looking out into the night. She must have been standing at a great height because Charl could make out the tops of trees below her. The woman was dressed for battle, but Charl could see no army. Instead, she saw behind her a large dragon, its hide so black it almost reflected the firelight. A horn or tusk protruded from its snout. The woman looked back over her shoulder at the dragon, and Charl saw fear in her eyes.

Not fear of the dragon, but fear *for* it.

Just as the image faded, a shrill scream ripped the silence.

18

RESCUE

Charl sat up in a panic, heart pounding. Her stitches pulled painfully, making her hiss with pain. The everlight burned steadily, and Prax had already scrambled to his feet. The scream still rang in her ears, but all was silent in the cave. Had she only imagined it?

Prax met her eyes and held a finger to his lips. He'd heard it too.

Charl moved stiffly to her feet and grabbed the lantern, following Prax to the edge of the shelf. Holding the light aloft, they looked out over the cavern below but there was nothing but glistening rock striated with patterns of white and yellow.

Charl fought an urge to run to the far end of the den and curl up in a ball where no one could find her. Whatever had woken them, she wasn't sure she wanted to find out.

But Prax was already climbing down the ledge.

"Hand me my pack," he said after he dropped to the ground.

Charl obeyed and passed down the lantern and her own spear.

"Wait." She stopped him after she dropped to his side. "I need some tea." She didn't add, *for whatever's coming*, but the look in Prax's eyes told her he understood.

The hendel was growing more bitter with time, but the pain in her back eased slightly and her mind grew more alert. Feeling less shaky, she shifted her spear to her right hand.

Another sound drifted out of the darkness. An urgent cry, but not the same scream as before.

Together they moved toward it, the rock beneath their feet ascending sharply. A pale light smudged the darkness ahead of them, and Prax picked up his pace, moving at a trot until they rounded the corner and stepped into the meager light of Wynne's lantern.

Charl gasped. Slip stood at the edge of a large pit, so wide and dark even the everlight couldn't penetrate it. A thick rope was wrapped around his waist, and his arms strained to hold it. His face was twisted in desperation and he leaned against the rope, trying to leverage his body against that of some powerful force on the other end.

Prax stumbled and swore, and Charl remembered how he'd refused to climb the rafters in the barn. But he steeled himself and moved to help Slip.

"Careful!" Charl called, seeing in her mind's eye

both men going over the edge. Prax stood to the side and grabbed the rope.

"Free yourself," he grunted to Slip.

"I can't," Slip said. "She'll fall."

Prax looked at Charl. "Your spear. Quick."

Charl handed him her spear, but he shook his head. "You'll have to do it. Twist it around the rope right here. There you go, just like that."

The rope was taut and resisted as Charl pushed the spear against it, but she managed to get one twist, then two. When she'd wrapped the rope around it three times, Prax turned to Slip.

"Now we'll grab both ends of the spear and pull. Ready?"

Charl stepped out of the way so the men could take the spear and, with great heaving groans, they pulled. Inch by inch, step by step fought with their heels digging against the rocky floor, they pulled the rope until at last a form appeared at the mouth of the pit.

Wynne's eyes were dazed and unfocused. She grasped weakly at the rope as the men hauled her up. When at last she was on solid ground, Prax and Slip collapsed onto the floor, panting.

"Thank you," Slip said, coughing from exertion. "I almost lost her. She slipped and hit the wall..."

Charl only had the hendel tea to offer Wynne, but the captain took it without complaining.

"You had a fall," Charl explained. "Drink this."

"My head hurts," Wynne said blearily. Her nose was swollen and bleeding, and a line of blood flowed red from her hairline down her temple and smeared across her cheek.

Slip reached in his pack for a dark vial and poured a few drops of liquid onto his fingers. "Don't bite me, Wynne," he warned as he rubbed the liquid against her bottom lip.

She grimaced and pulled away. "What is that? Get your dragon-sucking fingers out of my mouth, Slip!"

Slip shot his distorted grin at Charl. "Not too battered then, that's good. Lick your lips. It'll help, I promise. I've got to take a look at that cut." He pulled her hair away from her forehead to better see the wound. Her hair was matted with blood, but Charl didn't think the wound was deep.

Wynne frowned at Prax. "Don't let him near me. I've seen what he can do with a needle."

"Prax saved you, Captain," Char said indignantly. "If we hadn't come along when we did, Slip would have dropped you."

Wynne cringed, though at Charl's words or because Slip was rubbing a salve into her cut, Charl wasn't sure.

"It's true," Slip said gently. "I was about done in."

Wynne closed her eyes and breathed deeply as Slip rubbed in the ointment. He was so close to Charl, and the musty scent of his dragonskin cloak so overpowering, that she wanted to recoil. With great effort she held still so as to not jostle Wynne.

"I don't think I'll need to sew it," Slip murmured. "It's not very deep, just a graze. You're lucky."

Wynne cracked open an eye and looked at him reproachfully. "This is lucky?"

"Sure. You'll have a bit of a headache, but that should be it." He removed his dirty scarf and folded it deftly, then lifted Wynne's head and placed the scarf beneath it. Charl was surprised at his gentleness and wondered briefly how long Slip and Wynne had known each other.

Charl edged close to Prax, her gaze darting back the way they had come.

"I can't protect you if you don't stay with me," Slip said as if guessing her thoughts. His tone was mild, but clear. "This might have been avoided if you hadn't wandered off. It's not worth my time to hunt for you, but you should know that if she'd fallen, I would have. And it would have been best for you if I didn't find you."

"It wasn't our fault," Charl protested. "What did you think you were doing anyway? Sending her blindly into the pit? Do you even know how deep it is?"

Slip's expression darkened, his face shadowed as he bent over Wynne. "It was her idea, not mine. She doesn't like to be refused."

"I can believe that," Prax said. He was sitting on the ground looking at his hands, and Charl noticed red welts from the rope across his palms.

She crouched next to him and touched the welts gingerly, a question in her eyes.

He ignored her and pulled his hands away.

"Prax," she whispered. "Your hands. How can you hold a sword—"

"It's fine," he muttered.

Slip glanced at Prax's hands, and his expression softened as he understood. He held out the vial. "Here, just a few drops. We'll need it later when we face the dragon."

"Why?" Charl blurted before she could stop herself. "Why are you so interested in killing him?"

"This is what I do," he said simply. "And I'm good at it."

"But how can you live with yourself? Dragons are noble and intelligent creatures. They deserve an existence the same as you and me."

"Careful, farmer," Slip said, glancing at Wynne. But her eyes remained closed. "That sort of talk could get you in trouble. This man Larch? Wynne thinks he wasn't just trying to make a fortune with his illegal breeding. The dragon we're hunting—the one Wynne thinks Larch rented to your brother—is of particular significance. She thinks he might have been part of a movement to rejuvenate the wild dragon population."

Charl's eyebrows arched in disbelief. "Is that even possible?" Excitement flickered in her belly. All her life she'd wished she lived in the days of Meirdan when she could see the ancient dragons in their strength.

Slip frowned and lowered his voice even further. "If the last descendent of Meirdan the Protector were thought to have sympathies that direction, it would look really bad for you."

"I'm not part of an underground movement. But I don't want to see a dragon slaughtered needlessly, either. Don't expect me to support something that goes against everything my ancestors fought for."

To her frustration, Slip only smiled crookedly. "What exactly did your dragon farmer ancestors fight for? Agricultural independence?"

"They fought to make a space for dragons in our world, to allow us to exist together in harmony. That might not mean much to you, but it's a legacy I take very seriously."

Prax laid a hand on her arm. In warning or solidarity, she wasn't sure.

Slip stepped closer to Charl and looked her over with interest. "Don't you know why Meirdan was called The Protector?"

"Of course! She advocated for living peaceably with dragons and championed their usefulness and domesticity."

Slip shook his head. "She was called The Protector because her work was vital in hunting down and enslaving the last dragons. She protected *mankind*, making it so that we would never be threatened by wild dragons again."

Charl felt as if a hot poker were dragged across her middle. Just like that, with a few careless words, Slip had desecrated Meirdan's legacy.

"How could you say such a horrid thing?"

"Because it's true. Trappers like me train by studying Meirdan's work. She was fierce."

"The faerie sand is going to your head. Meirdan was renounced by her peers and sacrificed her career to champion peace between humans and dragons."

"And how do you think she did that? By studying dragons, learning their weaknesses to domesticate them, and teaching others how to kill those who wouldn't so easily give up their wills."

"You're wrong." Charl's ears felt hot, and she stepped away from Slip. "She was called The Protector because she stopped them from being wiped out. She cared about dragons. She wanted them to be preserved. She gave her life to save them."

"You're both right," Wynne murmured without opening her eyes. "And you're both wrong. Meirdan did protect dragons from extinction, but only the ones who could be safely domesticated. There were others who were too dangerous, too independent and cunning. For those, she shared her research with trappers and slayers so they could be eliminated. It wasn't the dragons Meirdan protected. It was humankind."

Anger rose like bile in her throat. How dare Wynne and Slip abuse the memory of Meirdan, the only thing Charl had left to tie her to her family? To give her life meaning and purpose? She turned on her heel and walked away from the pit, putting as much distance between them as possible. Hot tears pricked her eyes.

"You can't hide from the truth, Charl," Slip called after her. "The sooner you face it, the better."

Prax hurried to catch up to her. "If Slip has faerie sand, you know he'll be able to find us."

"I don't care," Charl snapped, wiping at her eyes.

"Why do those things upset you so much? What does it matter whether your however-many-greats-grandmother was exactly who you think she was?"

Charl turned down a side passageway and stopped when she was met with a wall of rock. She heaved a sigh of frustration and closed her eyes. When she opened them again, Prax was watching her, his brow lined with concern. How to explain?

"Before Roland left, back when we still went to market, did you notice how our stall was always separated from the others and kept very last of all?"

"I guess. I just assumed you liked the space."

Charl shook her head. "It was my father's idea to sell at market. He hoped to increase profits by selling straight to the villagers. He hoped the increased exposure would help us to gain more trust. But they just found a new way to put us in our place. Claimed that the smell was driving away their customers."

Prax snorted derisively. "The smell isn't that bad."

Charl's cheeks burned, and she looked away. "My point is, living with dragons means we're mistrusted and judged in everything we do. Being descendants of Meirdan the Protector gives us a noble reason for it. If you take Meirdan away from me, what else do I have? I've lost my parents. I've lost my brother. If I lose Meirdan, I have nothing. Might as well let the

Regs take my dragons and go somewhere else for a fresh start."

Except she knew she never would. How could she leave while Roland was missing? She couldn't risk him returning someday to discover her gone.

Prax leaned against the cave wall, the lantern light emphasizing his frown. He rubbed the stubble on his jaw in thought. "I understand the need for a fresh start. If you decide to give up this business for good, I can respect that. But don't do it because of something that may or may not be true about an ancestor that no one living today even knew."

But I do know her, she wanted to say. She knew they were just dreams, but somehow she still felt something she couldn't explain when she saw the woman in them. A connection that Prax wouldn't understand.

"I don't even know what to think anymore," she said wearily. "I'm sorry I brought you into this."

"It was my choice. You're not as alone as you think, Charl."

Looking into his eyes gleaming in the light of the everlight, she wanted to believe him. But when all was said and done, it wasn't Prax who carried the weight of Meirdan's legacy.

As if reading her thoughts, he added, "Maybe Meirdan was as honorable as you claim. Maybe she sold out under pressure. It doesn't really matter because you are not Meirdan."

But it does matter, Charl wanted to say. If she didn't know where she came from, how could she be sure about anything in her life? How could she be sure about her future?

Maybe it's time to stop looking for someone else to tell who you are and decide for yourself who you want to be.

The thought hit her so strong it took her breath away. But there was no time to consider because Prax was stepping toward her and reaching for her hand.

She jumped a little at his touch and hoped he didn't notice.

"I know you don't like it, but we need Slip on our side. If something goes wrong down there, he knows how to handle himself."

Charl pulled her hand away. "He's a trapper. He's paid to kill dragons."

"Which will increase our odds that we'll make it out alive," Prax said with half a smile. He looked as tired as she felt, but when he smiled...

Charl took a step back so she could breathe a little easier.

"I'm not killing any dragons today," she said firmly, then turned and walked away.

19
SECRETS REVEALED

Charl returned to the pit to find Slip inspecting the edge of a long sword in the light of the lantern. His brow was furrowed in concentration, but he spoke without turning as if he expected her. Had he heard her conversation with Prax?

"You asked me why I hunt dragons, and I suspect my answer didn't satisfy you," Slip said, his voice soft. "I'm not as callous as you think. I find much to admire in their species, and I'm not opposed to continuing to domesticate them as you do. It would be a shame indeed if they were to disappear entirely."

"Then why do you further their extinction?" Charl's voice seemed to carry out over the pit in spite of her efforts to match Slip's volume.

Slip turned and held the sword before her. "Have you ever seen an anstil blade?"

She stared at its gleaming copper-colored edge, not wanting to find beauty in it. But the everlight danced across its edge, drawing her eye to follow the line like a song. "I thought anstil was impossible to find."

"Impossible to make, yes. Meirdan destroyed her research on its creation before she died. But in her day, it was as common as steel yet far more effective in fighting dragons. Families have passed weapons forged of anstil down through generations. Surely you can respect such a family legacy."

His mocking smile barely registered to Charl as she stared at the blade. It was hard to focus on what he was saying, so entranced she was by the weapon. Forged in wickedness and suffering, her father had said. Requiring the death of a dragon, but only after great suffering. How could something so evil be so beautiful? And yet, it repelled her at the same time, filling her with a nameless dread.

"Anstil is a weapon unlike any other, giving a trapper a necessary advantage."

"Like faerie sand."

His scarred lips twisted. "Yes. Like faerie sand. I know what you're thinking, Charl. You're thinking that I come from a long line of trappers and inherited this sword as part of my birthright. But this sword didn't come to me from my father or grandfather. I earned it slaying a Shallowplate outside the borders of Lachlan."

"You expect me to be impressed?"

"I expect you to understand. Some of us have to earn our legacies for ourselves. My parents were farmers—not of dragons, like yours, but the common variety. If I wanted more than what they offered, I had to distinguish myself in a way that would rewrite my heritage and give me new opportunities beyond my parents' dreams."

Charl pulled her gaze away from the sword and looked into his eyes. He was standing so close, she could see flecks of silver in the gray. For a moment her voice was lost to her, and she swallowed to regain it.

"Ambition? If you think that is what I would understand, you don't know me at all."

"No. Not ambition." His low voice was almost intimate. He was so near; she wanted to step back but couldn't. It was as if she'd forgotten how to make her feet obey her will. "I'm talking of choosing to live your life on your own terms. Not to be bound by those who came before, forced into a role that they chose, but to discover for yourself what path you want to take. We are each given only one life. To spend it in the shadow of those long dead is hardly living at all."

Charl's words caught in her throat because somewhere deep in her chest a part of her hummed with the certainty of his words. Like something that had long been strangled was at last being given a chance to breathe.

"I'm not ashamed of my heritage," she protested. "It's not easy, and I'll never have great wealth or even know if I'll survive one winter to the next, but I'm proud of what I am. I wouldn't leave it behind to chase a comfortable life."

"It's not your dragon farmer heritage I'm talking about," Slip said meaningfully.

"That's enough." Prax's voice startled them both.

Charl stepped back, freed from whatever spell had held her.

Prax was standing behind her, looking at Slip with a dark fury.

"Prax, what's wrong?"

"Praxton knows all about escaping a heritage," Slip said as he sheathed his sword. His mocking tone had returned, the seriousness gone. "Ask him. See if he'll tell you the truth."

Wynne groaned and moved to sit up.

Slip crouched at her side, gingerly touching her face. She swatted his hand away like a biting fly.

"We've wasted too much time," Wynne said, but her voice was weak. "Have you found another way into the pit?"

Charl turned to Prax, taking advantage of Slip's distraction. "What's he talking about, Prax? Why do you two hate each other so much?"

Prax's frown relaxed. "We don't hate each other. We just disagree about...something."

"What's that?"

"It's you, Charlotte," Slip said mildly as he offered Wynne water.

"Slip!" Prax hissed. "You don't have the right."

"Maybe not. But if we're all going to face the dragon together, we can't have secrets and half-truths between us. We've got to be able to trust each other.

132

So you'd better tell her who you are right now, or I will."

Charl took a step away from Prax. "What does he mean?" Dread wrapped its cold fingers around her lungs. She stared at Prax, her neighbor of the past two years. Her friend. Her confidant. The man who had kept her from going mad from loneliness. His features that she'd memorized. Now, with a few words, Slip had turned him into a stranger.

Prax looked back and forth between Charl and Slip. His expression shifted from anger to resignation.

"You're scaring me, Prax," Charl said. "What does he know that I don't?"

In answer, Prax stepped forward and took her hands. "Charl, believe me when I say that you know everything you need to know about me. I've never lied to you about who I am. I just...didn't always tell the complete truth. Because to do so would mean telling you something that I swore I never would."

"What?" Charl's voice cracked.

"Your mother, Petrica of Sorcester, wasn't the daughter of a merchant. She was the daughter of a duke. The king's brother, to be exact. She gave up her birthright willingly when she married your father. That's how she wished it, and her family respected her choice."

A laugh bubbled into Charl's throat, but she choked on it, seeing that he wasn't smiling.

"That's ridiculous. I think I would know my own mother's history."

"I only know what your grandfather shared with

me. When the duke learned of her death, and that you and Roland lived on, he was concerned for you both. If you'd been young children, he would have brought you back to Sorcester. But you were both grown, and he didn't want to deprive you of the life you knew. He wanted to respect your mother's wishes for the life she chose for you."

Charl wanted to protest, but she held still, waiting to hear the rest of Prax's tale. He held her hands, his thumb rough as he rubbed it against her skin. Was he trying to soothe her or was it from his own nervousness? She couldn't tell.

"So the duke—your grandfather—asked the captain of the Royal Guard to send a trusted soldier who could go and watch over you, making sure no harm came to you both. As it turned out, the captain had a son who had always wished for a simpler life away from the city."

Charl snatched her hands away. "You?"

"I know it sounds like—"

"I was...an assignment?" Heat flooded her face.

"No! I mean, yes, but not how you make it sound. They wanted someone who could help keep you safe. They didn't want to interfere in your life here, your mother had been very clear about that."

"So you came to Ambrey and pretended to be a farmer? Pretended to be our friend? Pretended— dirty fangs, Prax, I kissed you!" Her hands flew to her lips in mortification.

"I never pretended. I accepted the assignment willingly. I never cared for Sorcester. I'm happy in

Ambrey. These past two years have felt more real to me than my life there ever did."

"But you lied. You knew all this about me and Roland, and you never said. We were all alone." Her voice broke a little as she thought of the despair she'd felt after Roland left. What if she'd known she had powerful family in Sorcester who could help? Maybe they could have done something. Her mother had talked very little about her family, and because her father's tales of raising dragons were so much more relevant to their lives, Charl had never asked. They hadn't even bothered to find her mother's family after she died. She felt a hollowness in her chest at the thought of her mother taking such a secret to her grave. How lonely she must have been. That was followed by a surge of anger. She shouldn't have kept it a secret. She and Roland had a right to know.

She turned that anger on Prax. "Why didn't you tell me after Roland disappeared? You know how hard it's been."

"I know, and I almost did. But I'd sworn not to, and I tried to help as best I could. I confess...a part of me has been afraid that you would leave if you knew the truth. That you would go to Sorcester and I would never see you again."

The warmth she felt at his words only stoked her anger. "Don't you dare. Don't you dare make it sound like...You lied to me. If you were truly my friend, if you ever cared for me, you would have told me the truth."

She broke away and fled down the nearest tunnel before the tears came.

"Leave her," Slip's voice carried from behind.

A part of her wished Prax would follow. Wished that she could feel his arms around her, comforting and safe. But she buried that feeling, angry at herself for being so quick to fall for him. She had fancied him from the first, but now she realized these past months without Roland had made her almost desperate in her loneliness. She'd been such a fool.

Slip knew. He'd recognized Prax last night when he met him. Which meant...

Charl thought back to Slip's taunting. Had he known who Charl was all along? Was her mother's story well-known in Sorcester? Or was Slip granted special access to the secrets of the powerful? Charl had never left Ambrey and had no idea how people lived in the great city. The thought that her grandfather and others could be living in comfort—while she ate shriveled turnips and spent dark winter evenings making each candle stretch—made her hate them all.

She walked blindly through the cave, not caring where she was going. Hating herself for being so gullible. Wishing she could find her way out of the cave and leave them all behind. Wishing she could get out of her own skin that felt like it didn't fit right anymore.

When she entered a spacious cavern, she paused, recognizing the large rockfall. She looked for the rock that reminded her of a cork popped from a giant bottle. The hidden crack was as she remembered it.

Large enough to walk through standing upright, but narrow enough that she could touch both walls on either side. Had it been chance that brought her here? Or had something guided her while she was too distracted by anger to notice?

She knew she shouldn't enter it alone. She should go back and get the others. She'd left her spear at the pit, so she didn't even have that to protect herself with. But something she couldn't name propelled her forward.

Holding the everlight before her, she rubbed her cheeks dry and stepped into the dark.

20

DAUGHTER OF MEIRDAN

Charl tried not to think of the heavy weight of rock overhead. But after a while, it was impossible to deny that the tunnel she'd entered—little more than a crack—was narrowing. Still she moved forward, committed to going as far as she could. After that...she didn't know.

She wanted to disappear. She couldn't face Prax again, not now that she knew the truth. Knowing he had played a role and deliberately lied about why he was her friend. Lied to her about her own history. His too, for that matter.

And she never suspected a thing.

The rock pressed closer and closer until she was forced to stoop, and then eventually to crawl. Then, abruptly, the ceiling dropped further. She stopped, resting her hands and knees. The tunnel continued, but she would have to slide forward on her stomach into the gap if she wanted to go any further. Her breath quickened just thinking about it.

What if she got stuck?

Sitting back on her heels, she closed her eyes against the light of the lantern and waited until her breathing slowed.

Daughter of Meirdan. You've come at last.

The words came with such force into her mind that she thought briefly that she'd heard them with her ears. Her eyes snapped opened, expecting to see someone near her, but there was only rock.

She closed her eyes again and tried to feel the words.

Where are you? she thought.

You're almost here.

The response to her question was so clear, her pulse raced. She hadn't imagined it.

Pushing the lantern before her, she dropped to her stomach and slithered into the gap. It wasn't a tight fit, but was close enough that she couldn't roll onto her side if she'd tried. The thought gave her a feeling of panic, but she pushed it from her mind. Instead, she pulled herself with her forearms as quickly as she could, anxious to get through it.

When there was no longer space for the lantern to remain upright, she hesitated. She reached her arm forward, and was relieved to feel open space. So close. She pushed the lantern forward on its side, and it rolled out of reach, the shield dropping and sending her into darkness.

Panicked at the sudden blinding dark, Charl exhaled and pushed one last time, tears coming to her eyes as the rock ceiling tore at the bandages on her back. She cried out with the effort and pain, but at last she was through. The narrow chute opened out, and her lungs expanded with relief.

Panting, she crawled out of the hole and sat with her knees tucked up in front of her. She dared not lean against the cave wall, her back throbbing as it did. With shaking fingers, she groped in the dark for the lantern.

The shield was hot to the touch, and she used her sleeve to protect her fingers as she lifted it. She blinked against the bright light as it flooded the cavern, trying to get a sense of the space. Rock formations littered the ground in front of her, like unfinished columns rising out of the floor. Damp walls stretched out to either side. Looking up, she couldn't see a ceiling, and instinctively she knew she was at the bottom of the pit that Slip and Wynne had tried to descend from overhead.

You bring stolen light to this place of shadows, a voice sounded in her mind.

Charl's breath caught, and she peered into the darkness. "Who are you?"

You don't know me, but I know you. Her blood runs rich through your veins.

An image of Meirdan formed in Charl's mind. She stood on a rocky promontory with a large cleft in the rocky cliff behind her.

"You knew Meirdan?" It staggered the mind. How old would this dragon have to be to have known Meirdan herself?

Humans have such a small sense of time. You do

not see what we see. I tried to explain this to Meirdan, but she never understood.

"How do you speak to me this way? What trickery is this?"

No trickery, little human. You've lived with our kind for so long, your mind is open. More than the male who brought me here.

"Roland?" Charl's heart skipped a beat. "You know my brother?"

Roland's face appeared in her mind, together with a heavily muscled man Charl didn't recognize. In the distance, Charl recognized the view of the back side of her farm and knew instinctively where they were.

The male's mind wasn't open enough. I tried to warn him. I told him to free me before the other men returned, but he was confused. He waited too long.

Charl saw an image of Roland dragged out of his bed in the dead of night by men with clubs and rope. She gasped.

"Is that what happened to him? Why did they take him? Can you tell me where he is?"

This is what I saw when the male left. I haven't seen him since. Only you.

"What does that mean? Please, I need to know where he is."

There was a shift in the darkness at the opposite side of the cavern. Charl stepped around a stone pillar. She wanted to see the creature she spoke with, but dreaded it at the same time.

"Will you reveal yourself to me?"

You ask many questions. I will answer what I can.

The darkness shifted again, and then light ran down the outer edge of a long curve. The form rippled and stretched, unfurling into a large wing the size of a ship's sail as the dragon stepped into the glow cast from the everlight.

21

DECISION

Charl's heart jumped to her throat. More than twice the size of her own dragons, the bull unfolded himself toward the open ceiling. He arched his serpentine neck and watched her with one shining yellow eye. The other was a hollow socket. On the end of his snout was a broken tusk that reminded Charl of Forest's eye tooth. He was the color of night and shadow, and where his scales glimmered in the everlight, she saw a hint of blue. Could it be that this was the same dragon she'd seen in her dreams of Meirdan?

"I think I know you. I've seen you in a dream."

What you call dreams are my memories. They do not bring me pleasure, but they're all I have in this place.

Her voice failed her. He stepped forward on legs as thick as trees, talons dripping with dragon oil. A faint clink drew Charl's attention to a large steel manacle attached to one leg.

"You're bound." She peered closer and saw where the manacle had worn a raw spot around his scaly leg.

That is the way of humans, to bind that which they fear. To control those whose power threatens their own.

"We must protect ourselves. Surely you can't fault us for that."

Protect yourself? Interesting choice of words, daughter of the one whom you call Protector.

Charl winced.

You defend her legacy. View her legacy now. It stands before you in chains.

"She saved your kind," Charl murmured, but she was less confident now.

She thought she could change the world, but all she did was hasten our destruction.

"She tried to protect you. She risked everything to be your champion."

We shared our secrets with her and she used them to destroy us. Once we ruled skies and mountains and valleys. Now our species is little more than livestock, stripped of power and enslaved to humans.

"It's not true," Charl whispered.

Truth is an excuse for humans to do what they will. I will show you truth.

The darkness of the cave was replaced by the scene of the woman standing near the campfire, more vivid than Charl had yet experienced. She stood in a wide stance, braced against an invisible foe, clenching a spear. Her face was grim as she looked over her shoulder at the dragon who crouched behind her. If words passed between them, Charl could not hear.

Charl felt as if she could reach out and touch her, so real she seemed. Was this Meirdan herself, making her last stand to protect this very dragon? Charl had always pictured her older when she gave her life to defend the last of the ancient ones. She'd imagined her as a wise scholar, raising her children and writing her history, defending them through words, not weapons.

Meirdan turned back to watch the deep shadows under the trees lining the slope. Shapes moved in the trees as dozens, maybe hundreds of soldiers broke out into the open and stopped before Meirdan, weapons raised.

She held her ground, one against an army. Charl watched with mounting dread, unable to turn away but not wanting to see Meirdan slaughtered. It was one thing to know that she gave her life for her work. More than a hundred years since, it was noble. But it was quite another to watch it happen. Still, she felt a sense of pride at watching Meirdan face her doom with unflinching courage.

And then, Meirdan lowered her spear. She stepped aside, moving to the edge of the firelight. The army surged forward, and the dragon tried to rear on its hind legs, wings flapping threateningly. But Charl saw now a collar affixed around his neck. A collar that glowed with a coppery sheen like anstil.

Horror gripped Charl's middle, twisting and squeezing so she could barely breathe. This was worse than if Meirdan had been torn to pieces. Instead,

Charl watched her traitorous ancestor stand aside and let the army take the dragon.

"No. This must be a trick. You're trying to manipulate me—"

She broke off as the bull arched his wings, sending a tremor along the leathery skin. She recognized the warning, though it was so much more threatening coming from the giant bull than from her own dragons.

Don't accuse me of deception to protect your own comfort, young human. Meirdan betrayed me that day, and denying it will not change what she did.

"I'm sorry," Charl said, though for which offense, she wasn't sure. She backed away until she felt the stone wall behind her back, her feet betraying her fear. The natural rock pillars were her only shield, and an inadequate one at best.

The dragon folded his wings and settled.

I won't hurt you, daughter of Meirdan. If I do, I will have to contend with the trapper, and the strength of my youth is long past. You're much more useful to me alive.

"Why?"

You have Meirdan's spirit. If you have her courage, you can do what your brother could not.

Unease swirled in Charl's belly. "What do you want of me?"

Free me. Your heart is not like others of your kind. You may be young but you have the courage to defy them. And your hands are small enough to open the lock.

Charl glanced at the shackle at his ankle. There was no visible keyhole. Its surface was smooth and unbroken.

"What will you do if I free you?"

Into her mind came an image of soaring over tree-tops and skimming along a cliff face through the mist of a waterfall.

I want to breathe fresh air again. I've been in bondage since Meirdan betrayed me. I've been chained to the earth, but I belong to the skies.

Charl looked overhead into the darkness.

"This is my home. If I free you, can you promise to go far from here and never come back?"

Again you show your small-mindedness, human. Never for you is only a few winter sleeps for me. It's been too many human lifetimes since I was last free. The world beyond is changed, and I would see it for myself before knowing where I shall call home.

"Does this mean you won't promise? I won't free you if you're just going to destroy my village."

The dragon's hide rippled as he crouched low, bringing his head closer. Charl backed against the cave wall, ignoring the sharp ache in her back. The dragon peeled his lips back to bare yellow fangs and snorted, bathing her in the smell of scorched flesh. He didn't open his mouth to speak, but his words were clear in her mind.

I will make no oath, human. An oath made in chains carries no weight. She who demands it has no honor.

Charl forced herself to look him directly in his

single eye, hoping that the stories were true and one who spoke with dragons could look them in the eye without inviting death. His pupils retracted to dark slits, and she held very still.

In his eyes she saw intelligence, so much more intelligence than her own dragons.

But not compassion.

Her voice trembled as she spoke. "I can't free you unless I know you won't hurt anyone. I won't risk starting another war between my kind and yours."

The dragon hissed and drew back, opening his wings in a whisper of wind.

You expect me to obey you like the cattle you keep as pets? I am the last of the Dwaillern, human.

Charl closed her eyes, her pulse racing, waiting for the agony of fire or a talon in her flesh. "Threaten me all you want, but don't forget that the Regs already know you're here. My best chance may very well be to give you to them."

The dragon growled, sending a primal shiver down Charl's spine.

You have not Meirdan's honor. When she betrayed us, it was to save her kind. She paid dearly for it, but it was a worthy end.

Charl saw it. She saw Meirdan watching as the great dragon was bound with chains. The anstil collar around the dragon's neck stopped him from using fire, Charl realized. But it was more than that. He moved sluggishly, his jaws snapping too late against the soldiers who drove spears into his flesh.

Charl cried out as a captain thrust his spear into the dragon's eye. Or was that Meirdan's cry?

Meirdan ran forward, shouting, with her spear raised against the captain. He turned from the dragon and drew his sword.

Soldiers grabbed Meirdan from behind, wrestling her to the ground. They pinned her to the earth and the captain stepped forward and drove his sword into her chest. Then he turned and walked away without another glance.

Nausea bubbled up in Charl's stomach, and she covered her mouth, watching Meirdan writhe on the ground, her blood soaking the grass. Meirdan's face was twisted in agony but her eyes followed the soldiers as they led the wounded dragon away. When the last of the soldiers had left, she lay there still. Alone, struggling to breathe, with blood pooling at her lips.

Charl sank to the floor. Her whole life she'd heard the tale of Meirdan's sacrifice. Never had she imagined it would have been so lonely and afraid. Never had she thought it was reaped from cowardice.

She thought of her father's pride when he told tales of Meirdan's noble work. She remembered countless hours poring over Meirdan's words as a girl, imagining how it would have been to join her as a champion for the ancient dragons. She never could have guessed that Meirdan was a traitor who was discarded as soon as she served no further use. Left to die alone in her shame.

Had her parents known that the legacy they sacrificed so much for was a lie? Surely Roland would have told her if he'd known. Or had he lied to her too? She'd loved so few people in her life, and she couldn't bear to think they'd all deceived her.

You can make this story right. Free me, and it begins today.

Charl took a shuddering breath and made her decision. "I will free you. Not because I'm indebted to correct Meirdan's wrong. Her choices were her own. But I am not Meirdan. I will not add to her wrong by continuing your captivity when I can end it."

Charl stepped forward hesitantly, the glow from the everlight running along the stone floor to end at the dragon's leg.

His talons glistened, and his musk was so strong that she wished she could cover her nose. But she wouldn't demean him further.

"You are a remarkable creature. I can see why Meirdan favored you above all others."

The chain clinked as he shifted his weight.

How do you know this?

"I grew up reading Meirdan's words. Often she spoke of a dragon of such intelligence that other dragons seemed inferior by comparison. It almost seemed as if they were friends. Maybe that was just a childish fancy."

My kind don't have...friends. But Meirdan was special. I grieved when she died, even though I knew she had wronged me most of all.

Charl reached for the lock and felt a sharp stabbing pain as a crackling filled the air. She yelped and pulled her hand back.

You live with dragons. You breathe the same air, your labor spent among their shed scales and waste from the time you were a hatchling.

"What does that have to do with anything?" She moaned, rubbing her hand against her trousers. It ached, and her fingers cramped convulsively.

A shudder rippled down the dragon's back. He stamped impatiently.

Most humans aren't affected by anstil. But you are different. It...won't be easy.

22

SAYING GOODBYE

The dragon loomed over Charl, his scent filling her nose. His scales showed the withering of age, but his talons could have eviscerated her before she blinked.

"What if I can't unlock you?" she asked, looking up into his single yellow eye.

Then you're not the human I thought you were.

"I never asked for this, you know. Before Roland disappeared, I always thought he'd be the one to stay and carry on being a dragon farmer. Not me."

She'd never said it out loud. But the act of speaking it made it true in a way that it never had been before, when it had existed as a half-formed thought quickly buried with guilt.

You think you have to choose your heritage before it becomes a part of you? Look at me here in shackles. Neither of us can escape what came before.

Charl's heart pounded in her chest. "What is your name? If I do this, I want to know your name."

You couldn't speak it if you tried. But Meirdan called me Graegyn.

"Graegyn. My name is Charl. Before I try to free you, I think you should know that." She flicked her braid over her shoulder. "And maybe...maybe you should know that the man I love is somewhere in this cave too."

Why would I need to know this?

Charl's throat tightened. "I don't know. I guess because...if something happens and I don't see him again, I feel like I should have told someone."

Graegyn lowered his head to the floor, blocking her path. Charl tensed and resisted the urge to take a step back. His breath was warm and stank of decay, his nostrils ringed with black.

My kind doesn't feel this love. Why would you feel something that brings such pain?

Charl lifted her chin. "Because it makes us human."

She stepped around him, striding forward in spite of the pounding of her heart. As soon as she grabbed the shackle, pain coursed through her hands and she dropped it. Setting her jaw, she reached for it again and cried out as the pain shot up her arms and into her neck. She held on, gritting her teeth against the pain until she dropped to her knees with the effort.

Slipping off her leather coat, she used it as a buffer between the anstil and her skin. Still her head buzzed and the anstil crackled as she turned it over to figure out how it worked. It appeared to be a simple mechanism, not requiring a key, but impossible for someone without human fingers to open. A pin slipped through the interlocking shackle much like a hinge, and Charl couldn't properly grasp it unless she used her bare fingers. But when she tried to slide it out, the pin wouldn't move.

The longer she held the lock, the more her hands burned through the leather. Panting, she tried again. Still the pin wouldn't move. With a yell of frustration and pain, she released it. Cradling her cramping hands, she looked up at Graegyn. Her chest was heaving as if she'd run a great distance.

"I'm not...strong enough. It's stuck. I can't move it."

The anstil clouds your mind and drains your strength. It is the same with my kind. The anstil weakens you and makes you believe you can't do it. You must try in spite of what you believe.

Charl remembered how she'd felt when Slip had shown her the anstil blade, as if she were caught in a spell. If the anstil affected Graegyn the way it did her, she understood why he'd been unable to defend himself against the soldiers during Meirdan's betrayal.

"I fear...I fear that I can't..."

You fear too much. You fear the wrong things. You fear yourself when you should fear those who put me in these chains. You fear me when you should fear your own kind. You fear your future when you should instead fear your past.

Charl shook her head, trying to clear it, but the dragon's words filled her with confusion. "You're trying to trick me, aren't you? There's more to this than you're telling me. What is it? What are you keeping from me?"

He shifted in agitation. *The properties of anstil don't usually affect your kind so strongly. You must truly be aligned with us, but how? What have you done? Have you absorbed a part of us into your blood?*

"Dragon oil," Charl realized. "I was wounded by one of my dragons."

His exasperation washed over her. *Then your suffering will be great.*

Charl bit her cheek against the pain and tried again, prying at the pin, trying to force it to move, but it remained stuck fast. Her hands ached and veins threaded up her wrists. She needed to open the lock. She needed to let the dragon go, but she could no longer remember why.

"It's too hard. It won't move for me."

Graegyn lowered his head to within inches of her own.

You will do this now, or I will roast you on the spot. And then I will send a flame down the tunnel you came from to roast the male who is coming after you.

"Prax is coming?" Charl lifted her head, the cloud lifting a little. "Prax could do it. Not only is he strong, but he doesn't live with dragons. It won't affect him as it does me."

The ridge along Graegyn's skull glinted in the light of the everlight, bone white and gleaming.

Why would the male help me?

"He..." She paused. She didn't want to tell

Graegyn about Forest. "He'll help me if I ask him. You must promise not to hurt him, though. He must be granted protection."

Very well.

Charl dropped the shackle and gripped the lantern to still her shaking hands. She found the tunnel quickly enough with the everlight and crouched at the space, listening.

"Prax? Are you there?"

"Charl!" His voice was muffled. "Are you all right? I heard you scream. Are you hurt?"

Charl looked at her trembling hands. "I need your help."

"I can't get through. The space is too tight. Do you know another way?"

"No. I don't." Charl sighed. Of course he wouldn't be able to fit. She had barely made it through herself.

Graegyn watched her. The shackle waited, taunting her with its promise of pain. If she couldn't open it, would the dragon carry out his threat against Prax?

Making a decision, she knelt by the entrance to the tunnel, pretending privacy even though she knew Graegyn could hear every word. "Go back, Prax. Go back and find your way out of the cave. There's something I need to do, and I thought you could help me, but you can't. The best thing you can do is get far away from here."

He didn't answer right away. "What's going on? What are you doing?"

"Don't worry about me. But please, for my sake, go."

"I can't. I promised to protect you, Charl."

The reminder of his deception steeled her resolve. "I don't need your protection. I *never* needed your protection. I only wanted your friendship. But it's no good to me now. Go. I can't do what I need to if you stay."

Another long pause. When his voice came again it was full of sorrow. "I never pretended what I feel for you, Charl."

She closed her eyes, thinking of the kiss.

"Goodbye, Prax."

There was no answer.

He was gone.

23
PULL THE PIN

Charl turned back to Graegyn, feeling drained. She needed her hendel tea, and some food wouldn't be a bad idea either, but both were in Prax's pack. Weak and shaking, she shuffled back to the manacle on the dragon's leg.

You are mourning.

"Maybe. I'll get over it."

Such a puzzling emotion. I've never understood why your kind weakens itself with such attachments.

"Be grateful," Charl snapped. "If I didn't feel human emotions, I wouldn't be trying to save you now."

You must hurry. The trapper is coming.

"How? I'm the only one who could get through that tunnel."

There's another way.

Of course. She still hadn't found whatever secret entrance Roland had used to bring the dragon into the cave in the first place. But Slip must have.

She was running out of time.

Charl glared at the manacle and straightened her spine as she reached for it again.

"Don't do it, Charl!"

Slip's voice rang out in the cave, reverberating against the stone walls. Charl looked for him, but could see no light besides her own.

Then she remembered, with faerie sand he didn't need a lantern.

Ignoring his command, she reached for the manacle. The pain was so intense that she cried out in spite of herself. She fingered the pin, trying to focus on it. Trying to keep in her mind the one thought that mattered.

Pull the pin. Release the lock.

Pull the pin.

Pull the—

Just as it started to budge, something knocked into her from behind, pushing her to the rocky floor. Charl cried out as her stitches tore, her eyes watering with pain.

"Stay down," Slip commanded.

"No, Slip! Don't hurt—"

But before she'd finished, Graegyn swiveled. His barbed tail whipped overhead, crashing into the nearest stone pillar and raining rocks over their heads.

Slip ducked over her protectively, and Charl coughed against the dust. She looked at her hand, surprised to see the pin laying in her palm.

She'd done it.

"Get out of here," Slip barked, grabbing his bow and slipping an arrow from his quiver.

Charl moved sluggishly to her feet, brushing away the rocks on her lap. She reached for the fallen lantern.

"Don't hurt him, Slip. He has a right to live the same as you and I do."

He grabbed her by the arm and pushed her into someone else's arms.

"Get her out of here. He's caught her mind."

Charl struggled against the newcomer's grip and only realized it was Wynne when she spoke.

"Come, Charlotte. You've done enough."

Why didn't Graegyn leave? She'd freed him. He got what he wanted.

Wynne pulled her through the rubble and past another pillar.

Charl stumbled, her eyes not on her feet but on Graegyn. He braced himself, shifting his weight to his back legs and—with a grinding sound like a bellows that needed oiling—expelled a stream of fire from his jaws so fierce that the air erupted with heat.

Wynne pulled her against a rock column, and they crouched together, cowering. Charl's skin felt tight from the heat, and she buried her face under her arms, seeking relief. A sound like an angry forest fire roared in her ears.

Slip.

She risked a glance around the column but couldn't see Slip in the flames. Heat waves shimmered in the air above the rock formations, illuminating Graegyn's hide and turning it a deep blue. Behind Graegyn, past where the chain had been driven into the rock, she could just make out an opening in the wall.

Roland's secret entrance.

Mere seconds passed before the fire ceased, but it felt like hours. When the fire stopped at last, the cave was left darker than ever. Charl tried not to think about Slip's charred body falling to ash.

This one cheats. He wears the skin of the dead.

The dragonskin cloak with the deep hood. It wasn't for dramatic effect. It was to shield Slip against dragon fire.

Charl breathed out a sigh.

"Slip?" Wynne called, a tremor in her voice.

Charl tried to see around the pillar, but wherever Slip was, he was hidden.

"Get to the passage," Slip called. "Take Charl with you. This one is half blind. It won't take long."

Go, Charl pleaded silently. *I freed you. Leave this place before it's too late.*

Graegyn didn't answer.

Wynne pulled Charl to her feet.

"Come on, farmer. We only have a few minutes before he can reignite." Wynne grabbed Charl by the shoulders.

Charl bit off a cry of pain. "My back. Please. You're hurting me."

Wynne loosened her grip but didn't release her. "Your life might not mean much, but I won't risk you getting in Slip's way. Now move."

Charl realized her hand was empty. She must have dropped the anstil pin in the rubble. There would be no binding the dragon again. Whatever happened now would end either with his freedom or his death.

Clearer of mind, she picked her way through broken rock while trying to keep an eye on Graegyn. The cave was so dark now, he looked black. She could just make him out in the everlight, crouching with his bony armored head nearer the ground, protecting his soft underbelly.

A movement caught the corner of her eye and she paused, watching as Slip darted behind a nearby pillar.

As soon as she registered he was there, Graegyn whipped his head that direction and lunged, teeth bared. He scrambled over rocks, and the natural pillars crumbled to dust under his weight. Jaws snapped as Slip disappeared under the rubble.

Charl gasped. Wynne pushed her out of the way, then drew her own sword and ran to Slip's defense.

"Get out of here, farmer!" she yelled. "You're giving the dragon an advantage!"

And then Charl realized that her connection with Graegyn meant he could see everything she saw. He'd known where Slip was hiding as soon as she'd seen it.

She froze, conflicted. She didn't want Graegyn to die, but she didn't want to be responsible for Slip and Wynne's deaths either.

She turned away and searched for the gap in the cave wall. It was a deeper shade of shadow against the black wall of the cave. Just large enough to get the dragon through if his wings were pinned.

Graegyn roared, and Charl looked back. An arrow was lodged in the soft underside of his jaw. Black blood trickled down his neck. He reared back and unleashed another stream of fire. Charl yelped and dropped to the floor. This didn't last as long as the first, but the chamber filled with heat, and when it stopped the air was filled with the smell of burning hair.

She blinked, trying to adjust to the sudden darkness. Shifting rock echoed in the cavern. Someone was moving. She peered into the darkness.

"Slip? Wynne? Are you okay?"

Another arrow fired from the shadows but this time Graegyn shifted and it glanced harmlessly off his ridged spine.

"Charl, you're going to get us killed." Slip's voice was urgent and strained. "Get to the tunnel. Now!"

Charl looked back over her shoulder at the gap in the wall. Fleeing now might be the only chance she had to survive. But then she remembered the way Meirdan had stepped aside, leaving Graegyn to capture. This fight would only end with the death of either the dragon or the humans, and if she left now, she would be responsible. It would haunt her for the rest of her life.

She couldn't accept that.

24

FREEDOM OR VENGEANCE

Graegyn's tail whipped forward, smashing into the rock pillars and collapsing them like a stack of child's blocks. Dust and flecks of stone bit Charl's eyes, making them water. She blinked, and as they cleared, she saw a blurry image of Slip and Wynne standing shoulder-to-shoulder, swords drawn.

They stood before the dragon in a space now cleared free of rock. No more protection.

Graegyn opened his jaws, but no fire came out. Instead, he whipped his sinuous neck to meet them with fangs bared.

"Stop!" Charl cried. She dropped her lantern and ran into the open space between the dragon and the humans.

Half of Wynne's hair was charred, leaving her skin blackened beneath. She looked as if she might drop on her feet but held her sword high. Slip's gray eyes caught the gleam of his anstil blade and he looked murderous.

"Please, stop! You don't know what you're doing!" Charl pleaded.

"You're going to kill us all, Charl." Slip sounded murderous too.

"Let's kill the farmer and be done with it," Wynne argued. "She freed the dragon, a crime of high treason. Her death is irrefutable at this point."

Charl turned her back to them and faced Graegyn.

"Do you hear her?" She spoke aloud so the others could hear her clearly. "Do you understand what it cost me to free you? If you die in this pit it will have been for nothing. You said I had no honor, but how much honor do you have if you waste my sacrifice?"

"Stand aside, Charlotte!" Slip shouted.

She waved a dismissive hand toward him, keeping her eyes on Graegyn. She imagined the scene he had shown her, of flying over treetops and soaring up waterfalls that fell from such great heights they disappeared into mist.

It's a bitter dream while my enemies live. I'm the last of the Dwaillern. My kind dies with me. I will kill the trapper while I can.

"Freedom. That's what you wanted. Not vengeance. You have a right to the first. But I won't let you seek the second."

You know they won't let me live. They'll slay me before I reach the sunlight.

Not if there's something they want more. Trust me.

She felt his hesitation as a whisper in her mind. A wavering ripple as he considered her words.

A scrape of boot on stone came from the shadows, and it took her a moment to realize it hadn't come from behind her.

When Graegyn whipped his head around and looked up at the cave wall, she understood.

Prax.

You think to use your male to trap me? This is a poor deception indeed. He's dangling like a fly in a spider's web.

"No! Prax go back! Please, Graegyn, I swear to you this isn't a trick."

"Charl!" Prax called. He swore loudly. "Does this pit never end?"

Slip darted out behind her, taking advantage of the dragon's distraction. Wynne grabbed Charl, pinning her arms.

"Our deal's off, farmer." Wynne spat. "Consider yourself under arrest."

Slip raised his sword to strike where his arrow had already found its mark.

She couldn't see Prax, but Graegyn's stare was intent as he crept closer to the wall. He arched his wings. The grinding sound of his fire igniting filled Charl with terror.

"The hatchling is alive!" she screamed.

Graegyn turned his single eye to her.

Slip paused in his strike.

"The hatchling survived. Please, there's more at

stake here—" She choked off as a cold blade pressed against her throat.

"You lied," Wynne hissed in her ear.

"Wynne," Slip warned. He gave a slight shake of his head. "Don't."

You speak of a hatchling now? Is this another trick?

"Let her go, Captain." Prax stepped out of the shadows, sword raised.

"There was a hatchling, like you thought." Charl spoke in a rush, Wynne's blade pressing harder against her neck. "I don't know if it's a male or female."

Is this true?

"Release her, Wynne!" Prax demanded.

Slip drew his own sword and stepped in front of Prax. "As much as I'd like to let Wynne give you a lesson in swordplay, this isn't the time. Stand down, Praxton."

"Where is the hatchling?" Wynne tightened her grip and Charl's neck burned. She craned her neck back and could only see empty darkness overhead.

"If you kill me now, you'll never know where it is."

"Then I'll tear your farm apart until I find it," Wynne growled. "I'll bring the full power of the Magical Regulation Squad down on your head."

The sharp sound of crossing blades rang through the cavern. Charl recognized Prax's grunt, and her knees felt weak. He had no hope against a trapper under the influence of faerie sand.

She swallowed painfully against Wynne's knife.

"And how will you explain to my grandfather why you killed me here instead of letting me stand trial in a proper court? Prax knows the truth. And Slip won't lie for you. Will you kill them both too?"

A sword clattered to the floor.

"Let her go, Wynne." Prax was breathing heavily.

Bless him for trying.

Wynne's grip relaxed. "You're the worst dragon-sucking farmer I've ever met, Charlotte." She released her with a push.

Charl stumbled forward and stared in shock. Slip was on his knees in front of Prax, his anstil sword on the ground. Prax's blade was at his neck.

Charl's eyes widened, unbelieving. Prax bested Slip?

Seeing Charl free, Prax dropped his blade and Slip collected his own with a dark expression.

Charl didn't have time to react before Graegyn's snout filled her vision. He peered at her, his wings still arched threateningly.

Do you speak true?

Charl answered silently. *You're not the last of the Dwaillern after all. Vengeance means nothing when you're dead. Hope is everything.*

If what you say is true, the hatchling must be protected. You must not let them have it.

Will you help me? I can't do it alone.

The last time I trusted a human, I ended up in chains.

"I am not Meirdan," she said fiercely, then paused, realizing she'd spoken aloud. She looked at

Slip. "What rights do I have through my mother's line? What protection might I claim?"

"What do you have in mind?"

"I don't want to be tried by the Regs. I want to make my case before the king."

Slip rubbed his jaw, considering. "That would be within your rights."

"And I want to do it with Graegyn at my side."

Wynne swore, and Graegyn's tail flicked.

You will betray me to them again, he said.

No. I will convince them. I'll plead for the hatchling's life by showing them that you deserve to live.

And if you lose?

Then we both die. But it's the best chance we have for your freedom and that of your offspring as well.

Slip pursed his lips. "You would lose faster than you could string a flock of pixies."

"Not if we stand with her." Prax sidled closer to Charl, and his fingers brushed hers. She gripped his hand gratefully.

"You're crazy if you think we would support this," Wynne said, moving to Slip's side where she could still keep an eye on the dragon. "Do you forget that Slip is Sorcester's most renowned trapper?"

"That's why his testimony would be so powerful." Prax said.

Slip was watching Charl closely. "What hold do you have on this dragon? Why does he not attack?"

"He's an intelligent creature. He can be persuaded as well as any human."

"Persuaded?" Slip frowned and looked at Graegyn. "Do you support this plan, dragon?"

Graegyn turned his single yellow eye to the trapper, his pupil dilating as he took him in.

Slip gazed back, unafraid.

Meirdan thought she could change the world. Perhaps her daughter actually will.

Graegyn lowered his head and folded his wings in submission.

"You can't seriously be considering this," Wynne insisted, looking at Slip. Her burned scalp was glistening. "You'll jeopardize your reputation. Your career. Our future."

In answer, Slip raised a hand to the side of her face that wasn't burned and brushed her short hair behind her ear.

"You know me. I don't risk what I can't afford to lose." He turned to Charl. "Perhaps it's time for a new legacy, Charlotte the Defender."

25
CHARLOTTE THE DEFENDER

Slip and Wynne led the way out of the cave, with Charl and Prax following. Graegyn came last, which had triggered a curse-filled objection from the captain. Slip had been calmer, but equally adamant against it.

"You realize it'll take one flame to roast us all and he'll be free."

"He's free now," Charl had snapped. "He's not my prisoner or yours. And since he has the best track record for honesty in this group, I'm inclined to trust him."

She'd turned to the dragon.

"Is there any point in asking you not to kill us?"

I'm weary of your requests for oaths. They are not given lightly, yet you ask for them as if they are slippery things, easily cast and just as easily cast aside.

"That's what I thought." She'd turned back to Slip. "We'll be fine."

As they made their way through the tunnel, Prax

held Charl's hand as if he were afraid of losing track of her.

"I wish I could have seen you best Slip," Charl said. "That must have been an incredible match. He even had faerie sand!"

"Well..." Prax lowered his voice and leaned in so his breath tickled the loose strands of hair against her ear. "I don't think he was trying that hard."

Charl looked ahead to where Slip and Wynne were walking. Slip had one arm around Wynne, who was moving at a shuffling pace as if every step pained her. He looked back over his shoulder at Charl and winked.

Charl stifled a laugh, and the warmth of it loosened a tightness in her chest she'd been feeling since first entering the cave.

Your male is right, Graegyn's voice sounded in her mind. *The trapper yielded too easily. Why? To gain your trust so that he can betray you?*

No. He was trying to save me. He was giving Prax leverage against Wynne.

Why would he do that? Where is the advantage for him?

He didn't do it to gain an advantage. He did it because he's human.

Daylight appeared at the end of the tunnel as a gray light drawing them with quickening steps like moths to a flame. The exit was littered with rubble, and the humans climbed over the boulders slowly while Graegyn managed it in a few short leaps. His movements were awkward and unsure, and Charl wondered if his depth perception was more hindered by blindness than she'd realized in the cave. Blood had dried the color of coal where Slip's arrow had penetrated his jaw. The arrow itself was gone now; Charl wasn't sure how he'd managed to knock it loose. But she was relieved because she didn't think she would have had the nerve to pull it out and she was certain he wouldn't have trusted any of the others.

Charl sighed as rock was replaced by blue sky and towering trees. They were in a deep depression, and an embankment sloped upward from the cave to a low ridge. Creeping vines in red and gold climbed tree trunks, and Charl breathed deeply, welcoming the fresh air into her lungs.

The ground underfoot was slippery with fallen leaves as Charl clambered up the slope after Prax. He stopped at the top and reached for her hand, pulling her up the final steps.

Charl looked around, shielding her eyes against the sudden sunlight. The wind was crisp and held a promise of winter snow, but for now the sun was shining in a brilliant blue sky. She tried to get her bearings. The mountainside fell away before them, and a ribbon of light below wound through the trees to a huddle of buildings.

Ambrey.

"How did I not know this was here? My farm is in the hollow right over there. I've set traps not that far from here."

"I expect it's hard to see the entrance from below. Roland must have known it was here."

One more secret he kept.

Graegyn spread his wings, and they rippled in the breeze, almost translucent against the light. Charl sensed his eagerness to fly. He could do it. He could burn Ambrey to the ground and soar away and she would be left to face justice alone. But he flexed his wings a few times, then folded them back against his body. In the full daylight, he was a deep indigo, and Charl wondered if Forest's color would shift to look more like his as he grew older.

I thought dragons preferred the dark, she noted.

We are creatures of the dark, yes. But after so many years even a dragon wants to see the sun.

Don't linger too long. The sun will have brought out the small game, and it's better fresh. When was the last time you had rabbit?

More years than you've watched the moon chase the sun.

My traps should be full, and my dragons won't be able to eat it all.

Graegyn shifted his head to look at her with his single eye. *I am not one of your pets.*

Of course not. You're a Dwaillern. But even a Dwaillern can enjoy rabbit.

He didn't argue.

Satisfied, Charl started down the hill with Prax at her side.

"I thought Wynne would arrest me as soon as I

stepped out of the cave," she observed, watching Slip and Wynne disappear ahead into the trees.

"I think she's not going to be arresting anyone anytime soon," Prax said. "She's injured pretty bad."

"Slip will take good care of her," Charl said, thinking of his many tinctures and ointments.

"Yes." A smile teased the corner of Prax's mouth. "I think he'll enjoy it more than she will, don't you?"

Charl smiled too, imagining Wynne submitting to Slip's ministrations. Theirs was a strange relationship.

She caught Prax's eye, and her smile died. There was so much that needed to be said between them, and she didn't know how to begin.

"Prax, I need a favor."

He raised one eyebrow questioningly.

"I need to know all I can about my grandfather. I'm going to need help making my case. Maybe he can even help me find Roland now that I have a better idea what happened to him."

Prax's expression grew thoughtful. "Of course. I suppose I should write to my father too, so he isn't surprised when we show up in Sorcester."

The silence between them grew long, and Charl watched her feet closely as she stepped over tree roots and mossy limbs hidden by ferns. She thought of Forest, of how to keep the hatchling safe, how to protect Prax, and what this might mean for the future of all dragons. She didn't dare mention any of this, though, not knowing how well Slip could hear them.

Prax broke the silence first as they entered a small clearing.

"Charl, I haven't had a chance to apologize. I never meant to hurt you. It seemed so simple in the beginning, but I was a fool not to see where it would lead."

Charl shot him a look from the corner of her eye. "You were going to tell me the truth the night I kissed you, weren't you?"

He ducked his head. "Yes. I'm sorry, I didn't mean to make you think—"

"It's fine. I understand." She said it breezily to hide the ache in her heart, hating herself for misinterpreting his motives.

"No, I don't think you do." Prax stopped walking and scanned the clearing. The others were out of sight. Even Graegyn hadn't followed, remaining instead on the ridge above the trees.

Prax closed the distance between them and lowered his voice. "I don't want any more secrets between us. But the most important one I haven't shared. I didn't jump into that pit today because it was my duty to protect you. No duty could have driven me to do that."

Charl smiled. "So your fear of heights is true?"

He shuddered. "I left my breakfast at the top if you need proof. I've never been so terrified. But I'd do it again if I had to."

"Why?" She needed him to say it, instead of filling in his words with her own imagination. She needed to know she wasn't letting her hopes run away with her.

He took her hands in his. "These last nine months I told myself I was just doing my duty, trying to be a good neighbor and keep you safe after Roland disappeared. But the truth is that I've been coming up with excuses to be near you. I convinced myself that if we continued as we were long enough, then eventually nothing else would matter. I could just be me and you could be you and that would be enough."

She swallowed, unable to look away from the intensity in his eyes. "That's always been enough for me."

He smiled. "Me too. I've wasted so much time, thinking there was no reason to rush things. And now I'm out of time. Everything is going to change. But I'll stand by your side, Charl, as long as you'll have me. And if you don't trust me, I understand. Just know that there will always be a part of me that yearns for that simpler life...with you."

His eyes flickered to her lips.

Charl could scarcely breathe. "Oh, Praxton. I don't know what I want. Everything is different now, and I don't even know who I am. But I can't imagine a life where I won't want you."

"Really? Do you mean it, Charl?"

She grinned at the relief on his face. "As long as you aren't going to tell me you're secretly a troll masked in human flesh."

He cocked his head and reached for her. "There's one way to make sure."

This time she waited for him to kiss her first, her skin tingling with anticipation. He ran one hand along her tangled braid and slipped the other behind her neck. He touched her so gently, it sent a shiver of need down her spine. He started at her forehead, just above her right eye, then followed her scar down her cheek, tracing it with his lips.

She closed her eyes, breathing in the scent of him —earthy and warm. She rested her hands against his chest, tentatively at first, then gripping his shirt and pulling him closer.

By the time his mouth found hers, she could think of nothing but him. Desire burned away every other thought, every doubt and fear. All she knew was his lips on hers, searching and warm, the roughness of his stubble, his hands sliding around her waist, pulling her to him.

Graegyn's voice broke into her thoughts. *I know this feeling. This is how Meirdan felt before she mated with her male. Are you going to mate with yours?*

Charl broke away with a gasp and staggered back. *No! It's just a kiss!*

Prax frowned. "Are you okay? Did I hurt you?"

"I'm fine, it's not..." She couldn't tell him. She would rather die first. Her cheeks burned with mortification.

Prax ran a hand through his hair. "I'm sorry, I got carried away."

"It's really okay. More than okay. And now I know you're definitely not a troll."

His eyes glinted. "You could check again, just to be sure. I really don't mind."

She laughed. "That's good to know."

"It's a sacrifice, but I'm here to serve." He grinned. "Come on, you need rest. Let's get you home."

Charl lifted her face to his for one last gentle kiss, then took his hand and let him lead her down the mountain. She glanced over her shoulder, spying Graegyn silhouetted against the sky, a hulking beast inspiring awe and ancient fear. But she felt only resignation.

This is going to take some getting used to.

Yes it is, Charlotte the Defender.

They walked slowly, wanting to make the moment stretch like the bands of light bathing the valley in a golden glow. The autumn colors were ablaze in the setting sun, and the river below shimmered like anstil. Winter would come soon, and with it a trial, meeting family she'd never known she had, and maybe even a reunion with a lost brother.

But for now, they had this moment. And it was enough.

THANK YOU FOR READING!

If you enjoyed this first installment of *Hatched*, please consider leaving a review on Amazon, Goodreads, or BookBub. Thank you for helping get my work into the hands of other readers like you!

For those of you who can't get enough of Charl and Prax, please enjoy a bonus scene that takes place between books 1 and 2. This exclusive epilogue is available to download when you sign up for my newsletter. And as a special perk, you'll also be the first to know when the next Hatched book is released!

Here's a short excerpt:

He tried to focus on applying the salve so his mind didn't wander to the softness of her skin or the curve of her spine or the way her hair brushed against her neck like an invitation.

The silence grew long with the only sound the snapping of the fire.

"Prax?"

"Hmm?"

"You're awfully quiet."

"I'm just talking to my dragon."

Charl snorted a laugh. "Is that right? And what does your dragon have to say?"

"He says that it's probably not smart to spend so much time alone with you. You're like a glory charm, and I can never get enough."

Find the full scene at carenhahn.com/farmer (or use the QR code below).

THE STORY CONTINUES...
HATCHED: DRAGON DEFENDER

Charl faces new dangers in Sorcester, where she must answer criminal charges for illegal dragon breeding. But someone doesn't want her to live long enough to make it to trial.

THE WALLKEEPER TRILOGY

She needs his help.
He doesn't trust her.
The battle of wills has begun.

"Brilliantly romantic and adventurous"

"a delicious, enchanting read"

"The intrigue, the excitement, the anticipation and fear, all makes you crave for more!"

"If you like Brandon Sanderson you'll love this."

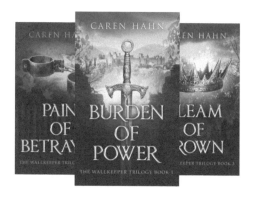

What do a high-octane mommy blogger, a Wild West romance, and a [possibly] possessed antique doll have in common?

You can find them all in my FREE collection of short stories. Visit carenhahn.com to download your copy!

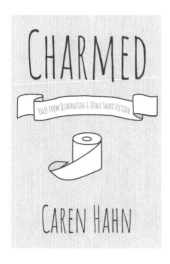

ACKNOWLEDGMENTS

Hatched began as humbly as you might expect for a light-hearted story about an orphaned dragon farmer who finds herself on the wrong side of the law. Inspired by a fantasy-themed writing prompt in the fall of 2018, I was struck with the thought of exploring a world where people raised dragons like we might raise chickens today. In fact, for a long time, the file was saved on my computer as simply, "Chicken Dragons." One scene led to another and with each writing camp iteration, I added a little more to Charl's story. It was an indulgence—a palate-cleanser between more serious projects—and for years it looked like it might never get finished.

Then Amazon launched its Kindle Vella serial fiction platform in the summer of 2021, which seemed like just the pressure I needed to finish Charl's story. After more than six months with Top Faved honors, I had two seasons completed and the seeds of a third. The serial format changed the way *Hatched* was written, too, and it was a great exercise to stretch myself in different ways.

My profound appreciation goes to those readers who discovered *Hatched* first on Kindle Vella and spread the word to fellow clean romantic fantasy readers. Word of mouth is so valuable in finding new readers, and I can't thank you enough for sharing.

Special thanks to Cathryn Schofield, whose All Day All Write camp is directly responsible for this story existing in the first place. And thanks to Rachel Stauffer, Crystal Brinkerhoff, Carli Schofield, and Hannah Hatch who enjoyed each installment even when I had no idea where it was going.

Thanks also to Rachel Pickett who not only polished it to a fine sheen, but asked important questions to make me think about the dragon lore I was invoking (or blatantly ignoring) for the *Hatched* world.

Hannah Hatch provided wonderful custom dragon silhouettes for the series covers when nothing else quite fit, even though their illustration skills are so far beyond this project that I felt embarrassed to ask.

And, of course, my husband Andrew was not only a vital part of the project as an early reader and cover designer, but also as the love of my life who infuses every romantic interaction in my fiction.

ABOUT THE AUTHOR

Caren Hahn specializes in crafting relationship dramas featuring empathetic characters who are exquisitely flawed—the stuff of great book club discussions. She writes primarily in the fantasy and mystery genres and is best known for her Wallkeeper Trilogy and Owl Creek Mysteries. No matter the genre, her richly layered plots and can't-put-it-down conclusions offer readers a thrilling ride blended with deep emotional resonance. Caren lives in the Pacific Northwest with her husband and six children.

———

Sign up for her newsletter to receive a free collection of short stories. Visit carenhahn.com to learn more about her upcoming projects.

Made in United States
Troutdale, OR
08/08/2024